the ghost who saved us

A.D. Ellis

one
brock shelton

"I'D LIKE to thank you all for coming so bright and early this morning," Bernard Lawson, an older man and owner of the old Prairie Brook mansion, said from the front porch steps.

Mansion was a bit of a misnomer for its current condition. The home had been built in 1898 by Presley Wade King. At the time, the home, which was built for his dear wife, had been massive and the most elaborate building for miles around. When she died during childbirth in 1900, the house and its owner had begun a slow decline. It was still a solid home, only needed some major TLC.

Which was why so many construction workers, carpenters, and contractors were gathered at the site at that moment. I hoped my bit of brief research, and being a local, would pay off. I wanted to be the one chosen to bring the home back to its former glory. I was so optimistic, I'd packed a bag in case I got the job and opted to stay on-sight.

"For those of you who traveled a long distance, I do hope you'll enjoy your stay in Prairie Brook. Only one of you will be chosen to work on this project today, but we'd like to invite you to stay a while and enjoy the town." Bernard, who had owned the Prairie Brook house since 1972—yet never actually resided in the place—smiled somewhat nervously at the gathered crowd. No doubt slightly shocked at the number of folks who showed up to place their bid on the restoration job.

"Now, as some of you may or may not know, I'm the owner of this beauty, but I'm currently working with Mr. Crimson Chaos to restore the home to its former glory." Bernard gestured toward the man cloaked in black standing next to him.

Crimson Chaos? What kind of name was that?

"So, without further ado, I'd like to introduce you to Crimson and let him share with you his vision for the Prairie Brook mansion. After he fills you in, we'll get down to business on taking bids." Bernard stepped to the side and the mysterious Crimson Chaos stepped up.

With a dramatic flourish of his black cape that had me biting back a snort, Crimson cleared his throat, lowered his dark sunglasses, and glanced at the gathered crowd.

"I," he began, loudly, and paused as if to wait for attention, "am the great Crimson Chaos. My vision for the Prairie Brook mansion is two-fold. It will be restored to its former glory and will bring business and money to Prairie Brook when I open it as a haunted hotel."

"Is it haunted?" a man in the crowd asked.

Bernard wrung his hands and looked as if he didn't want to answer, but Crimson gestured toward the large picture window.

"If reports are to be believed, this home is haunted by at least one, if not several, ghosts. While I haven't had the pleasure of encountering any of the spirits, I definitely feel their presence. Can you?" He slowly glanced around the crowd. "The home was originally built not only as a family residence, but also with plans to act as a funeral home."

A murmur went through the crowd and Crimson nodded, a smug smile on his thin, pale lips.

"Yes, a funeral home. Now, the home never met that goal as it was too far out of town to be convenient for a funeral home. However, the original owner, Presley Wade King, ran a mortician service and delivered bodies to churches and graveyards on a regular basis."

Crimson paused and rubbed his hands together, looking pretty much ridiculous in his black shoes, pants, shirt, cape, and wide-brimmed black hat in the middle of the small Midwestern town of Prairie Brook. He was just this side of too much for the little town and I had no doubt folks were already on the phone all across town talking about the strange, mysterious man.

A warm late-summer breeze kicked up and

Crimson adjusted his hat. "If a haunted work site is going to be a deal-breaker for any of you, I'd suggest you opt out now."

I watched a couple men make the sign of the cross and kiss the crucifix they wore around a chain on their necks before giving short waves, shaking their heads, and making their way toward their trucks.

"I respect their decision, this job will *not* be for the faint of heart," Crimson said, a ridiculous gravely quality to his voice.

Resisting the urge to roll my eyes, I studied the crowd again. About twelve people remained, mostly men, but a few women in the mix as well. I knew a couple of the folks in the group, but most were strangers to me. I wasn't sure if that was a positive or negative as far as me getting the job.

And then I saw him.

Calder Mills.

Holy.

Shit.

Calder and I had gone to school together since Kindergarten. We'd never been the best of friends, but we got along fine for the most part during our younger years.

In middle school, when I realized I was gay, Calder was the first and only guy, at least back then, my attraction landed on. We had a few random, hot and steamy run-ins throughout high school, all ending with Calder swearing he wasn't gay and threatening me if I told anyone.

Even way back then, I wasn't ashamed of who I was and I never denied my sexuality, but I would have never outed someone who wasn't ready. My crush on Calder never really decreased, but I finally admitted to myself I wasn't equipped to handle a secret relationship with anyone who couldn't be out and open.

I'd been on my own since I was sixteen when my parents died, but a few townsfolk made sure I was fed, clothed, and housed. I never missed school, worked damn hard at my job, and graduated with honors. Honestly, my parents—who were pretty much worthless drunks—dying was probably the best thing for me.

Calder and I finished high school and started our lives in Prairie Brook existing in each other's circles, but keeping our distance—a move I always figured was more on Calder's part than on mine.

I remembered the sting when I found out Calder left Prairie Brook when we were about twenty. I'd always got the impression he thought he was too big for the little town, but it didn't quell the irritation and emptiness I felt when he up and left without even so much as a goodbye or kiss my ass. Assuming Calder had been itching to leave town, probably trying to get away from his sexuality, looking to find deeper closets to hide in, had left me feeling sad and bereft.

I didn't know why.

It wasn't like the guy owed me anything.

Not like we'd *had* anything.

Except...

There had *always* been something different between Calder and me. A hotter spark? A deeper connection?

Sure, the few hot, secret blowjobs behind Old Man Mason's barn or under the bleachers during the football game had always ranked higher than any of my random hookups with other guys in town. But I'd chalked that up to Calder being adamant no one could know—the forbidden fruit and risk of being caught making everything all the more exciting.

But even at twenty-seven, no longer concerned about hiding behind barns or bleachers, the spark was still there the moment I saw the guy.

Whatever.

I cleared my throat and started to look away from Calder, but his eyes caught mine and held tight.

Damn, the man looked even better at twenty-eight than he had in high school. The tight gray t-shirt, worn work pants, loosely laced boots, and baseball cap were well-used and proved he was a hard worker. I knew he'd left Prairie Brook for a construction job and I'd always known him to be a man to do a good job. Was he back in town for good or just to throw in his bid on this project?

Forcing my blue eyes to break away from his golden-brown ones, I admonished myself for hoping he wouldn't get the job. I was happy in town with my friends, my construction business—I had special skills with carpentry and enjoyed dabbling in landscaping as well—and I wasn't going to be devastated if I didn't get this project. But my bank account and pride could do with a little padding and I really wanted to be the man chosen for this job.

And I really didn't need my head and dick getting all caught up on Calder Mills again.

"Now, if no one else feels the need to leave just yet, I'd like to move this gathering into the house to allow everyone a generous feel for the place." Crimson made a wide gesture toward the front door.

For a brief moment, I found myself making eye contact with Calder and suppressing a snort of laughter when we both rolled our eyes. Maybe I needed an entanglement with the guy like I needed a hole in my head, but that didn't mean we couldn't have a friendly connection thanks to the overly dramatic Crimson Chaos.

Once inside—which was dusty enough to jumpstart even the slightest of allergies—I took in the structure and automatically began cataloging things I'd like to do to restore the house.

When a shiver traveled through me and made the hairs on the back of my neck stand up, I mentally added a note to fix the drafts. Old houses were the worst for throwing money right out the drafty windows and doors.

Although…

I didn't give it much thought, but the day wasn't chilly, so the draft of icy air didn't exactly make sense.

Crimson pulled my attention from the thought.

"Now then, I don't know about the rest of you, but I'm immediately filled with bits and pieces of horrific terror upon entering this home. It will take just the right person to complete this job to my specifications *and* survive the creepy things I'm sure will go bump in the night." Crimson—who appeared to be doing his damnedest to convince people of just how haunted the house was—led us to a table covered in an old cloth and produced a box.

"Holy shit, man. Is that a Ouija board? Fuck no, man. I'm out of here," a guy to my left declared as he backed out the door.

"Nah, man, I don't play with that bad juju shit. I'm out." Another man followed suit.

"I need a job, but not that badly," a woman said, holding up her hands as if to protect herself from the board.

Crimson Chaos chuckled. "Well, that just made my job a bit easier. Our suitors are dropping like flies. Now, assuming the rest of you don't have a problem with me using the Ouija board to guide me in picking the right person for the job…" he trailed off and eyed us over the rim of his dark glasses.

While I would have rather been chosen based on my skills and qualifications, I had no issue with this odd man playing out his haunted mansion fantasies with his game board.

Crimson set up his board and asked us to all gather round. Right as he started a chant, another man threw up his hands and mumbled something about the situation being too damn weird before he left the little circle.

Mr. Chaos chanted and hummed for several moments before speaking. "Oh, great and honored spirits, show me the name of the chosen. The one to satisfy this home's longings and desires, the one to bring finality to my vision."

His hands rested lightly on the planchette. The heart-shaped pointer slid around the board and eventually spelled out C-E-M.

"Ah, our board has spoken," Crimson stated solemnly. "To whom do the initials C-E-M belong?"

Once again, the hair on the back of my neck stood up and a chill washed over me as Calder stepped forward.

"Calder Eric Mills," he said, looking almost sheepish to have been called out by the board.

Damn it.

As if it wasn't bad enough for the local boy to lose the job, I had to lose out to my old crush? Calder left town. *I* stayed. I built my business here and served the town. Not him.

While reminding myself not to act like a child who didn't get the toy he wanted, I gave what I hoped was a somewhat friendly nod of my head to Calder.

I wasn't ready for the spark of...was that interest in his eyes? I wondered briefly, while waiting for the little gathering to break up, if Calder would be down for a few old-friends-with-benefits situations while he was in town.

I wasn't looking for a closeted man to build a relationship with, but, as a small-town guy with limited options, I wasn't dumb enough to look a gift-horse in the mouth.

two
calder mills

Not gonna lie. As ridiculous as I felt being called out by a man named Crimson Chaos as he chanted and communicated with a Ouija board, I *needed* the job and I wasn't going to question the means by which I got it.

I'd left Prairie Brook about eight years ago—mostly, at least that's what I told myself back then, to get a decent job in construction. I'm mature enough now—and at least somewhat more comfortable with who I am—to admit I also left because I was terrified of the feelings I had for Brock Shelton.

Actually, I'd been terrified of the attraction I had for males in general—on television, movies, underwear packages, commercials that showed any type of abs, yeah, you get the picture. But it was the *feelings* I had for Brock that sent me running.

I'd slipped up and let a few random encounters happen between us and then freaked the fuck out after each one. After the first, our jizz was still warm on our hands when I sputtered it meant nothing and he couldn't tell anyone. The second, my spent cock had just slipped from his pretty mouth when I panicked. By the third encounter—when Brock greedily dropped to his knees and brought me off like a damn pro, leaving me reeling—even I realized how lame my excuses were sounding.

From that point on, I avoided any and all contact with Brock. We were in some of the same classes and it was impossible to not at least cross paths with the guy, but I made sure to never put myself in a position where my weakness for him would fuck me over.

Crazy to think about it now, but back then, my biggest fear was being outed. It seemed like the end of the world. Hindsight is twenty-twenty and all that, but at the time, it was a real fear.

So, I spent my days avoiding the one guy I could not get out of my head and my nights jerking off as I imagined his lips spread wide for me. Hell, we'd never even gotten past a shared hand job and him sucking me off, but my nightly fantasies were chock full of images of his gorgeous ass stretching around my cock.

He was a constant distraction and I was terrified of being found out.

Leaving Prairie Brook had been the best and worst thing for me. Worst because it landed me a job with a company I wasted eight years with. Best because it allowed me to grow up, face myself without an audience who'd known me my whole life, and finally accept the real me.

Yeah, maybe I hadn't told my parents about being gay.

Yet.

And maybe I wouldn't.

They were happy in Florida, entertaining friends, playing shuffle board, and living the retirement life. They'd been older when they had me and I'd never missed out on love and support, but I'd always felt a bit like an afterthought. Mom swore I was a blessing as they'd been told they couldn't have children, but it often seemed like they were just counting down the days until I was a legal adult and didn't need them to care for me.

I truly wasn't sure how they'd react to me telling them I was gay.

And it wasn't something I was ready to think about right then.

I'd just been chosen for a job that would allow me to branch out on my own.

For just a moment, I allowed myself to think back to Aaron. He'd been the first guy I'd wanted something more than secret hookups with when I moved away from Prairie Brook. Two years after moving away, I'd finally felt I was ready to be out and open, ready to date, possibly build a relationship. As much as I hated to admit it, I'd tried to forget Brock with Aaron. I hadn't been able to, but I'd truly liked him and wanted to see if things could go somewhere.

Imagine my surprise when Aaron refused to come out for me. There I was, finally feeling as if I knew myself—and *liked* myself—enough to face the fears and *be* with a man. No secrets, no hiding. At that point, I'd realized taking the job with the construction company had been a mistake, but I'd been tied into a contract at the time. I figured Aaron and I could do the whole dating thing for a while, and then I'd do something more with my career.

Little did I know at the time, Aaron was nowhere near ready to play the whole out and proud boyfriend. Neither of us had handled things very well and I honestly wasn't surprised when he left. It was for the best, but it still stung.

So, two years on my own, learning about myself.

Nearly a year struggling through whatever mess Aaron and I had.

And I was back in Prairie Brook after five more long, lonely, depressing years.

I felt older than my twenty-eight. The slight shimmer of silver at my temples and the beginnings of crow's feet around my eyes said I had a right to. Mom said I was beginning to look *distinguished* just like my father. I didn't love the hair—and there wasn't much to do about the wrinkles—but I usually just slapped on a hat and went about my day.

Part of me wanted to pretend I *only* came to Prairie Brook for the job opportunity. But a very large part of me *knew* I'd also hoped to catch sight of Brock. I tried not to make a habit of lying to myself these days.

But, Brock or no Brock, I was ready to tackle this

job—despite the ridiculous notion of ghosts and an obviously crazy backer in Crimson Chaos.

Where had the guy even come from? He was quite the character to be sure.

I tamped down the fluttery feeling in my chest at seeing Brock. Would he have any interest in seeing me while I was in town?

I wasn't under the impression I could stay in Prairie Brook. I had more bad vibes about trying to horn in on Brock's business than I had about the Ouija board picking me. But I'd be around for a while. I wasn't going to fool myself into thinking we'd spark up a forever—no matter how hot my blood *still* burned when I thought of our times way back then—but a couple hot-and-heavy nights between fixing up the mansion for Mr. Chaos sounded like a great way to spend my time.

Lost in thought, I couldn't help the shiver that traveled through me when what felt like a current of icy-cold air washed over me. The sensation was gone in a split second, but the hair stood up on my neck giving me the creeps. A hand on my arm caught my attention and I jerked to see who it belonged to, but no one was there.

Clearly, I was letting Crimson Chaos and his dramatics get to me.

Just as I was preparing myself to say friendly goodbyes to those who hadn't already taken off when their names weren't chosen, Crimson let out a strangled noise and pointed to the planchette as it slid across the board.

B

A

S

"The spirits have spoken," Crimson whispered. "To whom does B-A-S belong?"

I knew the answer in my heart before he even spoke.

"Um, Brock Ashley Shelton," Brock said, glancing around as if wondering if anyone else could claim the initials.

Crimson gestured for the two of us to step closer. As we moved toward him, I got the vague impression of the others leaving. Disgruntled grumbles and heavy footsteps were followed by an eerie silence.

Just when I expected Crimson to speak, he stiffened and his eyes glazed over as he stared at a spot behind Brock and me. Crimson murmured and nodded his head as if speaking to someone for several moments.

Brock and I exchanged glances with clueless shrugs.

Crimson took a deep shuddering breath and shook as he came out of his trance. "The spirits are pleased by this choice, but they have demands. Now, let's get down to the contract details."

As weird as the whole situation was, I wasn't going to argue a paying job and the chance to spend time with Brock. Sure, it was going to be hard-labor time spent, but beggars couldn't be choosers.

"Now, gentlemen, I'm going to bow out of this

conversation fairly quickly," Bernard said. "Mr. Chaos and I have our situation squared away. He'll share with you his wishes as far as the restoration and timeline. Any questions or concerns will be addressed to him." Bernard glanced around the old home. "I always had high hopes for this place, but it just never came to be. I knew if I held onto it for long enough, some good would eventually come from it. Turning it into a haunted attraction wasn't what I'd dreamed of, but if doing so will allow others to see the beauty of the home, I can't be disappointed."

We said our goodbyes to Bernard and took a seat at the kitchen table with Crimson. The furniture I'd seen so far was covered in cloths and I was itching to see what was under each covering. The house was over one hundred years old. Things definitely weren't going to be in pristine condition, but from the bits and pieces I'd seen so far, much of the house and belongings were fairly well preserved.

"Gentlemen, I'm quite pleased with the spirits' choices today," Crimson stated, templing his fingers under his chin. "The pay for this project remains fixed at the point stated in the original request for bids."

I fought the urge to point out the fact he'd kinda thrown the bid process all to hell with his game board drama, but I bit back my comment.

"However, I have monetary offers I'd like to share in hopes of enticing you." Crimson's face suddenly reminded me of every smarmy villain I'd ever seen on the big-screen and I almost laughed.

"Hang on," Brock interrupted. "That fixed price point you stated for the whole project is fine and dandy for *one* contractor. You're expecting us to split it? That's a crock of…"

Crimson held up a hand. "Mr. Shelton, you're very astute. While I can't and won't go against the spirits' wishes—despite the fact I'd planned on only one of you doing the job—I will offer the same base-price to both you and Mr. Mills."

Brock and I shared a shocked look, but the mysterious—and obviously *rich*—man in front of us continued.

"Now, I'm prepared to make some offers." Crimson rubbed his hands together. "This is my favorite part— the negotiations."

The man supposedly spoke to spirits and loved a good negotiation.

Weird just kept getting weirder.

"I will offer both of you a three percent bonus pay if you stay on-site during the project." Crimson raised his brows, waiting for us to respond.

I glanced at Brock and he shrugged. "Fine by me."

While I wasn't keen on sleeping in a supposedly haunted house, I wasn't going to turn down the money. I wasn't destitute, but the extra pay would definitely help pad my savings while I built up my independent business.

I nodded.

"Excellent. Having you on-site saves on travel expenses. Now, speaking of, I've provided a generous sum for gas money, food, and toiletries here." He slid a very fat envelope across the table. "And *this*," he added another even thicker envelope, "is for any and all materials you may need for the project. If it runs low, please let me know. And I do ask you provide receipts."

"Can do," Brock said with a nod. "What else?"

"I like an intelligent man," Crimson purred. "I know it will be a lot, but I'm willing to offer the base-price once over if you can finish the project in time for me to have the first tour come through on Halloween."

My eyes narrowed. "So, you're going to pay *him* the stated base-price, *me* the stated base-price, *and* pay us an additional base-price to split?"

Crimson nodded.

Brock frowned. "Before Halloween? That's like..." he paused as if flipping through a calendar in his head, "just over two months from now."

"The money is yours if you reach the goal. If not, you're not out your original pay. Consider it an incentive to work harder and quicker."

"We'll only shoot for before Halloween if we can do the work safely and well. I'm not okay with shoddy work just for extra money," Brock said.

"Agreed." I crossed my arms over my chest.

"I knew the spirits made a good choice," Crimson said with a demur smile.

"What if we need to get in touch with you?" I asked. No way was I starting a job with just a couple envelopes of cash if I didn't have assurances the source of that cash was reachable. Been burned before in the same type of situation. Okay, not exactly the same—because really, I was betting this was one of the strangest set-ups I'd ever been involved in—but I still wasn't going to let this guy just walk away with no contact information.

"Simply think of me and all will be provided," Crimson said.

Brock snorted. "Try again. We have a direct line to you or we walk."

Part of me wanted to slap an arm across his chest and tell him to shut the fuck up—I didn't need him making decisions for me—but I also agreed with his statement, so I kept my mouth shut.

Crimson sighed and slapped a worn looking card on the table. "Please only use it if there's a problem you can't fix or if the cash runs out." He stood up, adjusting his large sunglasses, black silk cape, and wide-brimmed black Fedora. "Now, gentlemen, I must take my leave. I've left my required fixes and requested additions in this folder. I'm sure you have much to discuss. I'd suggest getting your shopping done, get your supplies ordered, and have an early night so as to start bright and early tomorrow. You're officially on the clock with a lofty goal of finishing before Halloween if you want that extra money. Good day."

Crimson twirled around, flourishing his cape, and headed toward the front door.

Brock and I stood to follow, but when we reached the front door, the man was gone.

Just gone.

"What the hell…" Brock mumbled.

We walked out to the front porch. No vehicle, no dust, no Crimson Chaos.

"This may be the weirdest day of my life," I grumbled.

"Hell, man, don't go tempting the spirits. We're getting ready to take up residence in a haunted house, paid by a man who just disappeared, after we were *chosen* by a damn Ouija board. I don't think we need to challenge the paranormal to make things get any weirder," Brock said.

I couldn't help but chuckle. "True that."

We stood on the front porch for a moment before Brock broke the silence. "Wanna check our cash supply and get down to business?"

"Sounds good. Let's get started."

"In the spirit of moving past the possible awkwardness," Brock hedged, sticking out his hand, "it's good to see you."

I snorted. He had no idea just how good it was to see him, but I wasn't going to get into that right then. I took his hand, fighting the undeniable pull we'd always had between us. "Good to see you, too."

"You okay to be working with me?" Brock asked, eyeing me suspiciously.

"I'd work with the devil if it meant getting to do what I love and get paid for it."

Brock grunted as if not sure how to take my answer.

Honestly, I wasn't completely sure how I *meant* my answer.

But at least we'd moved past the initial awkwardness of not seeing each other for so long.

We spent the next hour poring over Crimson's specifications—which luckily weren't too outlandish—making lists of grocery and toiletry items needed, penning supply items onto an order pad as we thought of them, and casually chatting about the house.

"Damn it all to hell," Brock said as he ran a hand through his dark blond hair, his blue eyes snapping with irritation.

"What?"

"What are the chances the electricity got turned back on? No electric means no fridge, no microwave, no power tools."

My stomach sank. It wouldn't be the end of the world, but it would set us behind before we even got started if we had to wait for the electricity to be turned back on. Being way out in the middle of nowhere had made the old house pretty much untouched over the years, but it also meant getting the electricity to the house wasn't going to be as easy as just flipping a switch. Hopefully, Bernard or Crimson had already spoken to the electric company about getting the power turned back on.

"Well, at least the stove is gas. Bet the water heater is too."

"Not going to do us much good if we can't keep food cold," Brock groused.

"Nah, but we won't starve. And it's not the middle of winter, so we won't freeze. We'll get those chimneys cleared out and we can use the fireplace. Can even cook over the fire. Have our own little wiener roast." I wasn't usually Polly Sunshine, but I wasn't going to let a little thing throw off my day.

"No getting this job done by Halloween if we can't get power for our tools," Brock grumped.

I gestured toward the basement. "Let's check the breaker box first. No reason to borrow trouble." The very last thing I wanted to do was go down in that basement.

We made our way down into the dark, musty basement. It was old and smelled like a basement, but it wasn't wet or moldy, so that was a good sign. A wet basement wasn't good for many reasons.

"So, the house was built in 1898," I said. "The electricity would have been wired in later. Think Bernard did that? Or someone else before he bought it?"

"The records on the house are pretty non-existent from around 1920 to 1972 when Bernard bought it," Brock said, batting at a cobweb in the dim, shadowy basement. "Bernard seemed disappointed when he talked about the place. Like maybe he was upset he never lived here? But a lot of the appliances and furniture look newer—like when he would have moved in, even though he didn't stay."

"Yeah, everything so far seems to be a mix of the original stuff and then the addition of whatever

Bernard brought with him." I fumbled for my phone. The dirty windows let in some light, but not enough to see clearly. "He must have moved some things in before deciding not to stay. Or maybe he stayed for a short time and left thinking he'd be back? I wonder what happened to make him leave."

Brock made some kind of non-committal grunt. "Supposedly haunted. Remember the stories we used to hear about how the place had lots of ghosts—probably because of the mortuary. Always heard at least one ghost was pretty adamant no one stay around. But those were just stories we heard from older kids in town, no proof."

I shone my phone's flashlight around the large underground room and shivered when a current of icy air washed over me. "Basements creep me out. Check the breaker box."

Brock chuckled. "No need to be scared, I'll protect you," he teased.

Not that I *needed* protecting, but the thought of Brock's arms around me sent an unexpected zing through me.

He walked to the breaker box and opened it. Flipping the main breaker, he glanced toward the ceiling as if watching for something, anything. Suddenly, an electric hum filled the basement as a chest freezer came to life.

"Hell yeah," Brock declared with a fist pump. "Definitely don't want to look *in* that freezer just yet, but the fact it's running is good. Fridge in the kitchen is old, but we should be able to clean it up, plug it in, and get it running at least for a while. Only has to survive a couple months."

As we made our way up the stairs, I found myself stepping faster and slamming the door harder than was probably necessary when I swore voices whispered behind me from dark corners of the dingy basement.

"YOU SEE how much money is in here?" Calder whistled as he thumbed through the thick envelopes. "Definitely enough to stock our groceries and we're not going to be short on supplies, that's for sure. Damn, who the hell is Crimson Chaos?"

I chuckled "No idea, but if he keeps the money coming, I don't even care." I grabbed my keys. "Thoughts on keeping that money here versus putting it in the bank for safe keeping? I've got a bank account and we could use my card for purchases if you're comfortable with that set-up."

Calder glanced at the money and shrugged. "Hadn't thought about it, but it's probably not safe to have this type of cash around here. I trust you, let's use your account."

Hearing him say he trusted me did something funny to my stomach and I cleared my throat. "Sounds good."

From deep within the house, a clock chimed and I swear my entire body shivered.

"What the hell?" Calder shot me a look. "This place has been empty for how long? But a clock is still chiming?"

We made our way into the formal dining room to find an ornate grandfather clock. Clearly the source of the noise. But what caught our attention was the clock hands.

Clicking ever so slowly.

Backwards.

"The fuck?" I whispered.

"Gotta be a reasonable explanation, right?" Calder murmured.

"Mmhm. If ghosts wanting us out of here is *reasonable.*" I swallowed thickly. Could ghosts *hurt* you? They couldn't, right? Surely we could put up with a little jumpy creepiness for the amount of money we were making.

Calder looked around the room, a serious expression on his face. "You think they're mad? Looking for something? Like are they trapped here? Or just territorial and don't want us here?"

I shrugged. "Honestly, no clue. I don't have an iota of experience with paranormal beings. Hell, for all I know, maybe the spirits chose us for a reason."

"Like they need us to complete the project to open their portal to the other side?" Calder frowned.

"Your guess is as good as mine." I gestured toward the rest of the house. "Think we oughta check out the bed options? See what we need to make our haunted hotel stay more comfortable?"

Calder followed me from the dining room as we made a sweep of the entire house.

"One couch? That's it?" he groused after we checked each room.

"We'll get an air mattress and some blankets. Hell, we could sleep in the beds of our trucks while it's decently warm." We wandered back downstairs. I noted the house creaked and moaned as one would expect from an old house, but the foundation and building were firm and solid. The home had good bones that was for sure.

I gestured toward the door. "Wanna head into town for groceries? Grab lunch?"

Calder glanced around the place and nodded. "Maybe they need to realize we're here to do the job *they* picked us for," he said. "Maybe they need to stop being little bitches and let us do our job. We're not leaving," he said a bit louder. "So you can give up on that. Let us fix the place up and we'll be out of your hair."

"Maybe they don't want Crimson's haunted hotel? Maybe they just wanna live in peace?" It was weird to be talking about unproven ghosts as if they were real people, but the feeling had wrapped around me since the moment I'd arrived and made me think we were definitely dealing with something real.

Not something I'd ever dealt with.

Not something I *wanted* to deal with.

But real all the same.

We headed out the door and down the steps to my truck.

"You feel the drafts in that place?" Calder mused. "Thought for a while maybe it was just from old windows and doors. I don't know enough about ghosts, but don't they say you feel cold when ghosts touch you?"

Recalling the numerous cold chills across my skin during my time in the house, I tamped down a shiver. "Yeah, I felt them. Not sure about ghosts being cold. Look, I'm committed to seeing this job through, ghosts or no ghosts. You in or out? You need to decide now before we get too deep into things."

Calder narrowed his eyes and yanked open the truck door. "I'm in. One hundred percent. Not even sure I believe in ghosts, not gonna be run off by them."

I nodded. "Sounds good. I think we'll make a good team."

For the entire one-hour drive, we chatted easily—definitely keeping it very surface-level—about the things we'd seen in the house we wanted to fix and spruce up. We started a running list of the must-dos—some were items Crimson had demanded, some were our own ideas—and a list of want-to-dos—items we'd like to get to if the time and money were available.

"Lunch or groceries first?" I asked while we sat at a stoplight. Prairie Brook had a small grocery store, a hardware store, and a little coffee shop, but it had made more sense to head farther up the road to a discount grocery store and a much larger home improvement store. While it was just smart to help our money go further, I made note to be sure we spent a good chunk of our money in Prairie Brook—I always wanted to shop local if possible.

"Lunch first so we don't go overboard on groceries," Calder said.

I took a right and pulled into a burger joint that wasn't exactly fast food, but also wasn't what I'd call a sit-down restaurant. "This okay?"

Calder shrugged. "Fine by me."

We headed toward the door. From a few paces behind Calder, I was able to appreciate his broad shoulders stretched under the fabric of his t-shirt, a trim waist, thick thighs, and a gorgeous ass encased in worn denim. Whether he was still confused about his sexuality or not after all these years, at least I'd have some beautiful eye candy during this project.

After placing our orders at the counter, we took a seat at a booth in the corner and waited for our numbers to be called.

Figuring we had at least two months of working together ahead of us, I barreled right into conversation —and *not* of the surface-level type. "You come back to Prairie Brook *just* for this job?"

Calder studied me for a moment as if gauging how he wanted to answer my question. "Mostly."

I cocked a brow, but he didn't elaborate. "Leave a wife and two-point-five kids back home?"

Calder snorted. "Not quite." He leaned back in his

seat and crossed his arms over his chest. "We gonna have this discussion right here?"

"What discussion might that be?"

Calder huffed. "Right, as if you don't know."

I leaned in, elbows on the table. "Look, we've got a history in Prairie Brook and I don't want awkwardness between us on this job. If you've got something to say, say it."

"Pretty sure you're well-aware I had no interest in a wife and children. Not back then and not now. Left a tiny apartment, memories of a boyfriend who was a lot more like the old me than I was prepared to deal with, and a job I wasn't in love with. I'm back in Prairie Brook for this job." He held up a hand as if to stop my argument, even though I had absolutely nothing intelligent to say. "Don't worry, after this job, I'll head to another town. I'd never think of horning in on your business."

The speaker blared, "Orders fifty-eight and fifty-nine."

Calder glanced at my stunned face and smirked. "I'll get yours." He stood and strolled to the counter to pick up our trays.

What the ever-loving fuck had just happened?

Calder was gay?

I mean, I had his dick in my hand and mouth more than once back in high school, so I had a decent idea he was at least bi. But he was out? Had a boyfriend? Or *ex-*boyfriend from the sound of it. And now I was staying in a haunted house with him for two months as we restored the place?

I really wasn't sure which was more surreal, the potential ghosts or the fact Calder Mills had come out to me.

He returned to the table, placed my tray in front of me, and sat down with his own. Calder took one look at me and rolled his eyes. "You're not really surprised, are you?" he asked quietly.

I studied him for a moment, my head doing its best to wrap around our few hot and steamy encounters, his panicked insistence he wasn't gay after each of said encounters, the threats to keep my mouth shut, and the man currently sitting across from me openly mentioning a boyfriend and how he had no interest in a wife and children.

"You insisted you weren't gay." It was lame, but it was all my addled brain could come up with.

"I also sought you out to shove my dick down your throat when I could have easily had any girl in school on her knees," Calder said wryly.

"And you *did*," I shot back.

He ducked his head. "Yeah, and it's not something I'm proud of. I was definitely confused and scared back then. Thought if I *said* I wasn't gay enough times, it would maybe be true. If I got with enough girls, I'd eventually stop thinking about hot guys."

"Didn't work?" I asked, even though I knew the answer.

"Nope. Took me leaving town, being completely

alone with my thoughts for a while—probably helped I landed a job that reminded me daily of how miserable I was—before I finally just accepted who I really am." Calder shook his head and popped a fry in his mouth. "I swear, the moment I whispered *I'm gay* to my empty living room, it was like a weight lifted from my shoulders. From that point on, I promised to never hide the real me." He quirked a smile. "I'm not the type to announce my sexuality to every person I meet, but I'm honest if the question ever arises."

"And does it?" I asked, genuinely curious.

He shook his head. "Not much. Whether it's good or bad, a lot of people look at me and see a carpenter, someone who does a lot of construction jobs, a *man's man,*" he paused and rolled his eyes, "whatever *that* means. Folks don't peg me as gay. But I've been out in public on dates with guys." He shrugged. "I'm rambling. My point is, I'm not hiding in my closet anymore—but I completely understand and support those who are. I get that fear all too well."

He took a bite of his burger and we were both silent for a moment while we ate.

"Why did you tell me all of this?" I asked. Part of me was grateful for the truth, part of me was confused, and part of me was frustrated we'd missed out on a potential *something* way back then.

Calder was silent for so long, I wondered if he was ignoring my question, but then he finally answered. "Maybe it feels like I owe it to the kid I was all those years ago. Owe it to him to be honest and real.

Sometimes feels like I wasted so much time, never allowing myself to be the real me, and it makes me sad for who I used to be." He lifted a shoulder and took a drink. "But I know better now. Know myself better, know it's okay to be true to myself. Telling you just seems right—almost like it's giving that kid permission to be himself." Calder shook his head. "I don't know if that even makes any sense."

"No, it does," I said before finishing off my burger.

We were silent on the drive to the grocery store, but it wasn't an awkward silence, more like a comfortable silence where we were able to gather our thoughts.

A silence between friends.

Was that what Calder and I had?

Friendship?

A work partnership?

The possibility for something more?

Fuck.

For a brief moment, I thought maybe it would have been better if he *was* straight.

But then I caught a glimpse of his floppy dark-brown hair, golden-brown eyes, and scruffy chin.

No, I *definitely* didn't want this man to be straight.

But the question was, what the hell were we going to do with two months stuck together?

Oh, I had plenty of ideas about how I wanted to spend that time.

But was Calder on the same page?

Would mixing the job and pleasure be a recipe for disaster?

We spent an hour in the grocery store, filling our cart with staples to keep in the pantry, plus ingredients for meals, quick lunches, and breakfasts.

"What were you going to do if you didn't get this job?" I asked Calder as we roamed the health and beauty aisles.

Calder didn't answer immediately and I caught him eying the condoms and lube. My mind immediately went to the items I'd thrown in my travel bag as a *just in case* last minute addition. While it had been a while since my last sexual partner, and I'd had negative test results between then and now, I'd always made sure to have supplies if needed or requested. While I hadn't been sure I'd get *this* job, I knew I'd be on the road for a while, so I'd packed accordingly.

Was he thinking about potential ways for us to pass time between restoring the house and fending off ghosts?

He cleared his throat. "Um, figured if I didn't get this one, I'd move on. There are some towns similar to Prairie Brook in the area that don't have a carpenter or general contractor. Thought about figuring out a way to drum up some business there."

My eyes went wide. "So, you just left your home to move from town-to-town in hopes of setting up a business?"

Calder shrugged. "No, I left home to get this job." He winked and I was quickly reminded of how cocky he could be as blood zipped toward my cock. "My contingency plan was to move town-to-town."

The words were out of my mouth before I could even think them through. "Maybe we see how this project goes first, but I'm gonna be completely transparent and let you know I've been thinking about bringing on a partner. We make this job work, maybe we chat about combining our forces?" The weirdest part about my mouth spilling words without my permission was I wasn't even upset. The thought of working with Calder didn't freak me out—I'd known him as a dedicated, talented, hard worker way back then, and my gut told me nothing had changed about that over the years.

When Calder narrowed his eyes and studied me as if waiting for the punch line, I gave a shrug. "Just keep it in the back of your mind. Let's see how this job goes first."

If I'd been spending my own money on our purchases, I would have nearly gagged when the total flashed on the register, but it was a fraction of the amount Crimson had given us, so I didn't even bat an eye.

After loading my truck with our haul, we stopped by the bank and deposited the money into my business account before heading to the home improvement store.

Three hours later, completely dragging ass, we unloaded our groceries. After filling the fridge—which was beyond old but luckily still functioned—and pantry, we pulled out the sheets and blankets we'd bought.

"You wanna do an air mattress and the couch? Or try the truck beds while the nights are still warm?" I asked, yanking tags from our new bedding while wishing we had a washer and dryer available. I wondered briefly if we could get an old pair in here and set them up just to save us time driving to and from the laundromat.

"This place feel different to you?" Calder asked, not answering my question.

I glanced at him and caught the way he frowned as he looked around the room.

"Different how?"

Calder shook his head. "Don't know. Just different than when we left."

I followed him to the living room, grunting in frustration as I slammed into his back when he stopped dead in his tracks. "What the fuck, man?"

"Guess that's my answer." He gestured toward the king-sized bed sitting directly behind the couch.

"The fuck?" I mumbled. "How'd Crimson get that here so quickly?"

"How do we know it was Crimson?"

I ran a hand over the silky, soft comforter stretched across the bed. "Guess we don't. Do spirits have a direct line to mattress manufacturers and delivery trucks? And who provided the sheets? These are expensive," I said, running my hand over the buttery-soft sheets at the upper corner of the mattress.

Calder narrowed his eyes and stared around the living room as if looking for someone to blame. But after a moment, he shivered and shook his head. "Let's just agree to believe it was Mr. Chaos and leave it at that."

"So, we don't need the air mattress," I hedged.

Calder grabbed the sheets from my hands. "I'll take the couch."

"You sure?"

"You want it?"

I chuckled. "No. I'm not taking the couch when there's a crazy-nice bed right here. I'm just saying, the bed is huge, I don't mind sharing."

Calder looked as if he wanted to take the offer, but he cleared his throat. "Nah, the couch is fine. We've got the fireplace right here, I'll stay warm enough."

A twinge of disappointment traveled through me, but I wasn't going to beg the man to sleep in my bed. "Okay, well, offer stands." I wrinkled my nose. "Little weird to be sleeping in the living room, but I guess beggars can't be choosers."

"Let's move the bed to the master bedroom." Calder glanced around the room. "Actually, let's move the couch *and* bed in there. We're going to be doing a lot of work out here, it would be best to keep our beds away from the dust."

We took about twenty minutes to move the bed and the couch into the main bedroom on the first floor. Then we hung our clothes in the closet and placed our personal items on the built-in shelves.

"Glad we both packed some things before heading to bid on this job. We'll need to do a few things to spruce this room up, but it looks better than the rest of the house. Almost like Bernard fixed it up in preparation to move in, but then never really ended up using it."

Over the next hour or so, Calder and I eventually stopped jumping at every creaky floorboard overhead. The slamming doors were a bit harder to ignore, and the rattling doorknobs bordered on overkill.

"You think it's worth letting them know we're friendly? We're not here to displace them, just to make the place a bit nicer? Maybe easier to get through this job if we're on friendly terms," I mused, glancing around the bedroom as I swore shadows moved.

"You hear that?" Calder asked the room. "Brock and me go way back, we're friends. We're not here to hurt you. We just wanna do our job and get out of your hair. Maybe if you could lay-off the haunted shit and just let us do our work?"

A current of cold air moved through the room. We definitely weren't alone. Had the ghost—ghosts?— heard what we said? Were they watching us? Planning an attack?

Was their presence why Bernard had never taken residency in the home? They'd run him off?

"We need to check the chimneys tomorrow, make sure they're safe for us to start a fire in here. Not terribly cold at night just yet, but we'll get some cool temperatures pretty soon," Calder said as he plugged his phone into a battery pack.

"I've got a Wi-Fi box. I'll give you the password so

you're not eatin' up data. Probably better check the wiring—it's not my specialty at all, but I can spot red flags if I see them." I set my phone to charge before going to the attached bathroom to wash my face and brush my teeth.

"I'm pretty decent with electric work, I can probably fix any small problems. I'm guessing Bernard had the place wired when he thought he was moving in. So, not super up-to-date, but I doubt it needs complete replacing. If it does, Crimson will need to deal with that on his own." Calder moved about the bedroom as he spoke.

We switched places then. Calder, dressed in a t-shirt and lounge pants, took the bathroom and I moved to the bedroom to change out of my work clothes. Used to sleeping in just my boxers, I shrugged and climbed into bed in my usual state of dress.

"Really, the bed is huge. Don't feel like you have to sleep on the couch," I offered when Calder returned to the bedroom.

"I'm good," Calder answered shortly, his eyes roaming quickly over my bare chest and to the blankets gathered at my waist as if wondering what I wore—or didn't wear—under there.

"What time you want to get started?" I asked with a yawn. The day had been long—a mix of getting a lot done and seeming like we'd not actually *done* anything.

"I'd like to be started by six. That work for you?"

"You making me coffee?" I teased.

"I'll make coffee if you make breakfast," Calder shot back.

I chuckled. "Toast and eggs are about the limit of my breakfast repertoire. I can do pancakes and bacon, but that's only for special occasions."

"Good thing we got plenty of frozen breakfast items and that little microwave." Calder stripped off his shirt and pants, giving me just enough of a glimpse of his gorgeous body to make me need to bite back a groan. Then he covered the couch cushions with a sheet and a blanket before lying down and stretching two more blankets over himself.

I reached for the bedside lamp and clicked it off, plunging the room into complete darkness. "G'night."

"G'night," Calder answered around a yawn.

"You sure you're comfy there?"

"Yep, be even better when the fireplace can be used. I'll be all fancy stretched out on my couch in front of the roaring fire."

We fell silent, listening to the normal sounds of an old house out in the middle of nowhere.

And the not-so-normal sounds of a *haunted*—maybe that wasn't the right word, maybe it was simply *occupied*—house out in the middle of nowhere.

Not knowing the house at all, some of the sounds were difficult to discern. Was that popping noise just the house settling at the end of the day? What about that creak? Surely, the howling noise was just a coyote off in the distance.

Right?

At some point, I must have finally fallen asleep because I woke with a start.

The room was chilled and I was grateful for my warm blankets. We'd definitely need to make sure the fireplace could be safely used soon; the nights were getting a lot cooler than I'd originally thought.

What was that noise?

It took me several moments to realize it was Calder's teeth chattering.

"Oh my god, you stubborn ass. You're freezing. Get in this bed and get warm," I demanded.

Calder rolled from the couch, bringing blankets with him, and shuffled to the bed. "Swear the ghosts are punking me. It's like having an ice blanket wrapped around me. Why aren't they messing with you?" He continued to shiver as he crawled under the blankets.

"Maybe they're romantics and want us in bed together? Maybe they realized I was the smarter one so they only fucked with you until you came to your senses? I don't know. Just go to sleep. Morning will be here way too soon." I curled to my side, facing away from Calder, hoping sleep would engulf me quickly. The thought of Calder next to me had me on edge. I could totally sleep in the same bed with someone without mauling them, that wasn't the issue.

But memories of brief, sloppy kisses, fumbling hand jobs, and rushed, messy blow jobs filled my head, making me wonder if the tiny spark we'd had between us back then could possibly still be there.

I pushed the thoughts from my head. I wasn't there for rekindling a physical attraction.

Too late, already flamed to life.

Fine, but I wasn't here to find the love of my life. I had a job to do. I didn't need to get all up in my feelings over some guy I had a thing for way back in high school.

Calder was gay.

So, what?

Didn't mean we were meant to be together.

Don't try to kid yourself. You're into him, just as much as you were back then, if not more. This has second-chance romance written all over it and you're totally here for it.

I huffed and shifted, doing my best to get comfortable.

Only when Calder's shivering stopped and his breathing evened out did I finally drift off to sleep.

four
calder

I WOKE UP TOASTY WARM. After the freeze-out on the couch the night before—I swore the spirits were blowing their icy breaths on me, or covering me so I'd feel their cold, or *something*—it was a glorious feeling.

I also woke with a warm, cuddly Brock curled into my chest, my arm protectively around him, his head tucked perfectly under my chin as if we were an established couple who slept in intimate bliss every night.

Fuck.

I wasn't sure which hit me like a punch to the gut harder, the fact things were about to get awkward or the fact I liked having him in my arms so much.

It would be weird to be bed-buddies and friends-who-cuddle with the guy I was restoring a house with, right?

I let my mind drift back to the few brief encounters

Brock and I had in high school. Guilt and regret wrapped around me.

Adult me realized those two teens weren't ready for a real relationship and we likely would have crashed and burned even if I had been able and willing to be true to myself. But that angsty teen me of the past still yearned for what might have been.

The past may be gone, but the present is right here, wrapped in your arms. Maybe even the future...

Taking a deep breath, doing my best not to wake Brock so I could enjoy the moment just a bit longer, I savored the scent of the man in my arms. Faded shampoo and soap tickled my senses, but the underlying scent of *just Brock* stirred something deep inside.

Longing to tip his head up and kiss him—*for real* kisses, not the quick, lead-to-the-good-stuff kisses of so long ago—caress my hands down his back, cup his ass, rock my raging morning wood into him, capture his sexy grunts and groans with my mouth...

Fuck, man. Get it together. You slept in his bed for warmth, nothing more. Just because he got you off a few times in high school doesn't mean he's looking for anything now. You're here to do a job. Period.

Brock's words from the day before ran through my head. Would he really be willing to bring me on as a partner in his business? Did his thoughts on the offer include us having a business-only relationship? Or had he let his mind wander to how we could possibly make a real relationship work while running a business together?

I had to admit, the thought of owning my own business, getting to do what I loved day-in and day-out, working with a man I could easily see my heart getting all tangled up in…it was enticing as hell.

But the what-ifs and risks were real.

If Brock and I didn't work out, would he rescind his offer?

If we crashed, would our working relationship suffer?

Could we keep our personal lives separate from our business lives?

Fuck, Mills. You're thinking about shit that hasn't even happened. So what if the sexiest man you've ever seen is curled in your arms after suggesting maybe you go into business together? Just because he rolled next to you during the night doesn't mean he's ready to choose font and embossing for wedding invitations.

Brock shifted in my arms and I felt the tension the moment he realized he was curled into me. Wanting to make things as easy as possible, I pretended to just wake up. "Shit, sorry about that, must have been colder than I realized," I said, loosening my embrace, immediately missing the close contact of his warm body.

Brock cleared his throat. "Yeah, same. No worries. We've been in more compromising positions." His words came out joking—he was trying to relieve the tension as well—but they only served to remind me of how hot and sweet his mouth was all those years ago. How hard he'd made me, how quickly we'd both come.

And so help me, how badly I wanted to do it again.

Wanted to kiss him, stroke him off, take the silky weight of him on my tongue, and suck him dry.

Fuck.

I rolled from bed and quickly made my way to the bathroom trying to escape my thoughts and get my dick under control.

I wanted Brock.

Badly.

The desperate desire burning in my gut for the man was the exact reason I'd left Prairie Brook all those years ago. Back then, I hadn't been able to deal with how badly I wanted him—physically and beyond—so, I'd run.

In the grand scheme of things, me running off had been for the best. I liked the person I was a whole lot better these days. But running off had done nothing to tame the fire in my blood for him.

Now, I was back home, a whole lot more comfortable with my sexuality, and working alongside the object of my desire every day for at least two months.

And sleeping next to him every damn night if the shithead ghosts had anything to do with it.

Is it really an inconvenience to sleep next to him? Maybe the spirits did you a favor.

I couldn't help the grin as I brushed my teeth.

Maybe we had some romantic, match-making ghosts in our midst.

As I took a quick shower, I admitted to myself working with Brock, sharing his bed, and maybe —*possibly*, if fate was smiling on me—getting to see if that tiny spark from way back when might grow into something more, wasn't a hardship.

Making my mind up as I dried off, I decided I'd not only be open to things happening between us over the next two months, I'd take it one step farther by letting Brock know I was interested.

As badly as I'd wanted to rut our cocks together and start the day with mutual orgasms, I promised myself I'd take things slow. Maybe get him talking about the past, gauge the situation—hell, a sinking feeling washed over me, did Brock have a boyfriend?

Why hadn't the idea of Brock being involved with someone crossed my mind sooner?

So, step one was coffee and breakfast.

Step two, find out if Brock was involved. Lick my wounds and deal with it if he was.

Step three—between restoring the house and dealing with ghosts—make it known I wanted to give those teens from so long ago an actual chance.

After that?

Well, there were a lot of *if then* scenarios that could play out, so it seemed best to take it slow and see where things stood after step three.

If I even got to step three.

Shit.

It hadn't even occurred to me he might have a boyfriend. Hell, maybe even a husband. I hadn't seen a ring, but people in our line of work often didn't wear rings.

I sighed.

Okay, so I had some goals.

Between the work, the ghosts, and hopefully romancing Brock, at least I wouldn't be bored.

Brock and I easily fell into a smooth working relationship. Honestly, it was as if we'd been working together for years. We were perfectly in-sync with how we wanted to accomplish Crimson's goals, plus our own ideas for making the house shine, and we never ran out of things to chat about as we worked.

Hell, we even had similar tastes in music so our days were filled with tunes, laughing and joking, and bringing a gorgeous old home back to—and beyond—its original glory. We'd thrown together a playlist from circa 2013 when we'd been seniors in high school and the music kept us bopping throughout our work.

I'd come back to Prairie Brook for a job and a new beginning, and a tiny seed of hope had taken root deep in my soul. Surrounded by sawdust, carpentry tools, a good song in the air, and spending time with a man who had quickly regained the top slot on my favorite persons list, I allowed myself to believe things were maybe, just maybe, looking up.

With an unspoken agreement, we continued to sleep in the same bed. It truly was ridiculous to sleep on a couch when there was a whole-ass bed available. Brock didn't seem to mind and I'd decided there was no reason *not* to.

Our morning wake-ups also fell into a routine. We'd go to bed each night on the farthest edges of the bed, but each morning we'd wake in the middle, curled together. It made me smile to think of our sleeping forms being pulled together throughout the night—never satisfied until our warm bodies connected, relaxing into each other, relieved to be touching, safe, *home*.

Yeah, maybe I was being a bit overdramatic about it. So, what? We were cuddlers, it didn't have to be a big deal. But it felt like a big deal. Hell, even Aaron and I hadn't slept cuddled together the few times he'd slept over.

Going to bed was nice, but waking up was something I quickly came to look forward to. I wasn't gonna lie, I had high hopes we'd eventually add a bit more action to our nighttime and morning routine.

In addition to our work and sleep, we also adapted to the spirits in the house—or rather, *spirit* as we'd determined it felt as if there was really only one ghost. Or at least only one who was mingling in our space—maybe there were others, but they weren't causing any disruptions. We'd quickly settled into the home enough to notice things we'd not noticed earlier.

Yes, there was definitely a spirit among us. Too

much happened that could only be explained by accepting something supernatural shared the home with us. Tools were moved, doorknobs rattled, windows slammed shut, and the lemon-scented candle we'd picked up on our grocery trip constantly got snuffed out.

But none of these things happened simultaneously, which led us to believe we were dealing with only one spirit.

And as we learned the house and got more acquainted with our ghost, Brock and I both agreed nothing felt dangerous or deadly. We weren't scared for our lives or afraid every noise would bring something evil.

No, our ghost was a pain in the ass, but he—she?—wasn't evil. Bored, maybe? A bit of a brat seeking attention?

"How long do you think he's been here?" Brock mused one day while we worked to finish the counters in the kitchen.

I shrugged. "House was built in 1898, right? Bernard bought it in the seventies? So, we can assume the ghost has been here since sometime between 1898 and 1970-ish since Bernard ended up never living here."

Brock stood in the middle of the room, hands on hips—looking like a cross between a damn carpentry magazine model and the beginning of a porn you know is going to be stupid as hell but so damn hot—and pursed his lips. "Can't even imagine what it would have been like to live back then. I'd love to see photographs of this place when it was first built. I wonder what the people who lived here were like. Is our ghost one of them?"

I smiled as I put the finishing touch on the countertop I'd been working on. I loved Brock's mind. So many times, blue-collar workers got pigeon-holed into being good with their hands, but not having a lot of intelligence, and that was pure bullshit.

Not only was Brock highly skilled and talented in our trade, he was also a thinker. I knew he'd done some research on the house. "Didn't you look up some information about the place?"

He nodded. "Yeah, Presley Wade King built the house in 1898 for his wife. She died in 1900 during childbirth."

My brows shot up. "Maybe she's our ghost?"

"Maybe," Brock answered absently.

Stepping closer, I stood directly in front of him. "You okay?"

He shook his head as if pulling himself from a trance. "Yeah, sorry. Just got to wondering about the family. Were they happy? Was it scary to live in a mortuary? Did the baby grow up here?" He huffed. "Just lost in my head for a minute. It's easy to see this place as just a project, a paycheck, but it struck me this house has seen birth and death."

Brock turned and pointed to the living room. "Maybe a kid played in there, fell down the stairs and busted their knee," he gestured toward the backdoor, "played outside on warm summer days, climbed trees."

When he turned back toward me, we were closer than we'd been before. Close enough I could have reached out, wrapped my arm around his waist, and pulled him in close. I knew what he felt like in my arms, knew the press of his broad shoulders against me, knew the warm scent of his skin.

And I wanted to experience it outside the bedroom.

Experience it for real.

Not just waking up curled together, something we could laugh off and ignore, but *real*. Because we wanted to touch, to explore, to claim.

Without warning, an ice-cold presence pressed against my back and I went tumbling forward. With a grunt, I grabbed for Brock to steady myself.

His arms immediately caught me, keeping me from falling. "Whoa."

And just like that, we were face-to-face, tangled together. With anyone else, I would have stepped back, out of his space, but the temptation to be close to Brock was too much.

I allowed myself to stay right there, my back still tingling with cold shivers from whatever had pushed me. Because something did push me, there was no doubt in my mind.

Or *someone*.

I smiled.

"What?" Brock asked, an eyebrow cocked.

"Anyone else would think I'm losing my mind and

tell me I was just clumsy, but I swear our ghost just pushed me so we'd end up like this."

"You felt him?" Brock scowled. "I keep saying *him* and I don't know why. It's like my gut feels it's a man."

"Felt him as real as I can feel you right now." I paused, shifting my arms slightly, but not untangling us from our loose embrace. "This okay?"

Brock's blue eyes sparked with desire when they met mine. "I'm good," he answered gruffly. "So, what? Our spirit wants us together?"

I shrugged. "I have absolutely no clue. Maybe we can spend some of our off-the-clock time digging into the history of this place? Figure out who we think he is?" I glanced around the room, getting the feeling we were definitely being watched. "Don't they say ghosts stay somewhere if they can't crossover for some reason? Maybe we can help him?"

Brock smiled. "I'd like that. Nothing feels *bad* about this place, but I keep getting bits and pieces of feeling sad. Almost like," he paused, chewing on his lip, "like despair? Longing? Resigned?"

Looking around the room, wishing I could see our ghost, I nodded. "Yeah, I get that. Maybe he'll figure out he can trust us to help him. I don't know why he's stuck here, but he's probably been here anywhere between a hundred and a hundred-twenty years. I can understand the despair."

Brock snorted.

"What?" I frowned.

"Just thinking he's probably right here in the room.

I wonder if this is the most action he's seen in a century."

I froze. "Between two guys? You think he's offended?"

Brock tightened his arms around me. "First, he pushed us together, right? I doubt he's too offended. Second, just like back in high school, ask me if I give a fuck what someone thinks about me."

Smiling, I took a step forward and pushed Brock into the corner of the cabinet, loving the grunt of appreciation escaping him when our hips connected firmly.

Desire flashed in his blue eyes and his nostrils flared with want.

I dipped my head and ghosted my lips over his, holding my breath as I waited to see if he would deny the kiss.

Brock huffed a happy little chuckle before gripping the back of my neck and pulling me down to deepen the kiss.

My insides melted as the soft warmth and familiar flavor of his mouth engulfed me, bringing happy memories back to the forefront of my mind.

This man had always had the ability to set me on fire.

And I'd run from it.

But no more.

I groaned into Brock's mouth and wrapped him more tightly in my arms, rocking our hips together, wanting to freeze time and savor the moment forever, but also wishing we could move things along.

My dick was most definitely interested in that option.

A scratching sound from behind us caught my attention right before the scent of a burning match filled the air.

I turned our entangled bodies, my lips pressed against Brock's temple.

"You're seeing that, right?" Brock murmured.

"Our candle being lit by a matchmaking ghost? Yep, I see it."

"Is the candle his peace offering? Now that he pushed us together, he's going to stop being *such a pain in the ass*," Brock spoke loudly to the room, "and let us keep our candle burning?"

"If keeping him happy means kissing you, I think I can deal with the inconvenience," I whispered against his ear, loving the way Brock shivered in my arms.

"We have a lot of work we need to be doing," Brock half-heartedly protested as he shifted in my arms and hovered his lips over mine, warm breath tickling my skin.

"We do, but we also have a spirit friend who seems to want us in compromising positions." I nuzzled my nose into his. "Maybe we give him the kisses he wants and then we work?"

Laughter flickered in Brock's pretty blues eyes. "I like that plan."

And then he brought our lips back together and I was lost.

Those few kisses from so long ago didn't hold a candle to the confident warmth of Brock's lips against mine now. Slick heat, needy grunts, and unspoken promises of how much better everything between us could be sent hopeful desire coursing through me.

Just as I was close to ripping our clothes off and taking him to bed—trying my best to tell my head to fuck off with its internal warning that maybe I was moving too fast—tires on the driveway sounded and interrupted like a bucket of ice water.

Brock sighed as our bodies separated and I mourned the loss of his warm strength against me. He moved to the large picture window.

"Well, I'll be damned."

"What?"

"If it's not a case of our very own meddling spirit interrupting our work, it's an old man with an ancient television walking up our drive to interrupt...other things," Brock said, a smile in his words even as he watched out the window.

I joined him and saw Bernard wrapping a cord around a small, old TV and making his way toward the door.

Moving from the window, I opened the door and took the TV from Bernard.

"You come bearing old appliances?" I joked as the man huffed and brushed dust from his shirt.

"Well, I was cleaning out my garage and came

across this beauty." Bernard thumped the television. "Plugged it in to be sure it worked. Not gonna get any streaming services on it," he chuckled at his own joke, "but it should pick up a couple local channels with this converter switch and antenna, even if it's just the news. Figured you boys might need something to keep you occupied when you're not working."

A brief image of a naked Brock, spread open beneath me, groaning my name as I pressed deep into his body flashed through my mind. Pretty sure we had plenty to keep us busy, but the gift of the television was thoughtful all the same.

"Thanks," Brock said, moving to clear a spot on the counter. "We've got our phones, but it does get pretty boring out here with nothing else to do when we're not working." He threw a smirk and a wink my way, my dick thrilling with the knowledge our thoughts had likely gone to the same place.

"Well, I won't keep you boys from your work." Bernard brushed his hands together as he glanced around the room. "Looks like you've gotten quite a bit done." The old man sighed. "I bought this place for pennies and big dreams. For the longest time, I refused to let go of it because it meant letting go of the dreams I had."

"Tell me to fuck off if I'm being too nosy, but why didn't you stay here?" I asked.

A brief shadow washed over Bernard's face. "I couldn't handle the spirit." His eyes caught mine and he nodded. "I'm sure you've had a few run-ins. He seemed to be angry I was here and my wife, God bless her soul, she wasn't having anything to do with a haunted house in the middle of nowhere. So, while I dreamed of settling in and filling the place with love and children, Anna told me we were living in town or else she was living somewhere without me." He shrugged. "So, I paid a bit here and there over the years to keep things safe—wiring and such—and had the house aired out and somewhat cleaned from time-to-time, but mostly it's just sat here wasting away. Filled with stories of sadness and pain, never getting to live up to its potential and be filled from the inside out with love of family."

Something about his statement lodged in my heart. "Do you know who the ghost is?"

Bernard shook his head. "Could be the mother who died here. Could be the father—stories handed down over the years say Presley Wade King killed himself, found dead by his son, Presley Allen King at age eighteen. The stories of the son aren't very clear, but he died here too is my understanding. Could be him. Could be one of several individuals who were treated within the mortuary. Really no way of knowing."

We walked Bernard around the house, showing him projects we'd already completed, the ones we were working on, and the ones we had next on our list. As we headed down the front steps to Bernard's truck, he ran a hand through his thinning, silver hair.

"You boys get any wild hairs to go gathering information, there's a secret room in the basement. It's where Presley senior had his mortuary. Also kept a collection of sorts. There's a box. I never had the nerve to go back down there after the first time I found it, so I have no clue what's in the box. But I'd rather the two of you go through it than Crimson find it and exploit the secrets of the past." Bernard climbed into the truck and slammed the door. "Lookin' real good out here, boys. I truly do hope this place can finally find peace; maybe it won't ever experience love, but I guess peace is the next best thing."

Bernard's words stayed with me as Brock and I set about making sandwiches with turkey, ham, salami, bacon, and cheese on thick soft slices of bread. We'd agreed early on to eat our perishables first and save the more stable items for later.

"You think he's right?" I asked.

Brock cocked an eyebrow as he popped a chip in his mouth and washed it down with a swig of craft beer.

"Bernard. Saying this place may never experience love?"

He shrugged. "If the man built it for his wife, he likely loved her. They got a little time here before she passed." Brock glanced around. "Not sure about the father and son, sounds like sad stories all around."

"And here we are helping fix it up so it can become some sort of sideshow attraction? Not sure it sits right."

"You backin' out?"

I shook my head. "Nah, just thinkin'." Taking another bite of sandwich, I tried to push away the cloud of melancholy. "You stayed in Prairie Brook all this time? Never tried to get away?"

Brock chewed a bite, swallowed, and nodded. "Been here the whole time. Where was I gonna go? I had my parents' house and the business from Dad—he may have been an alcoholic, but he somehow kept a business running fairly smoothly. After high school, I took over and there's never been a thought of leaving. I'm a small-town boy and I'm happy here." He cocked his head. "Your parents still in Florida?"

I chuckled. "Yeah, don't see them coming back. Dad hated the snow. Mom is president of her euchre club down there."

"They know you're...gay? Bi?"

Clearing my throat, I shook my head. "No."

Something clouded over Brock's features.

"I don't see them often and I don't feel like it's a phone conversation type thing. Honestly, their knowledge of my sexuality really doesn't change anything. I'm gay and them knowing or approving—or not—has no bearing on who I am."

Brock nodded. "I get that." He smirked. "So, this boyfriend you mentioned..."

"Aaron. Good guy. I convinced myself I could be happy with him and we fell into a relationship pretty quickly. But I was at a point where I wanted to take him out, show off what we had, celebrate who we were, and he was *not* in the same position." I brushed a crumb from the table. "I'd spent too long hiding and wasn't ready to go back into the closet—even though I completely understood where he was coming from. For a time, kinda felt like karma was raining down on me, ya know?" I shrugged. "We parted on fairly friendly terms." Didn't seem like the time to mention I'd basically tried to fill the empty Brock-shaped spot with Aaron and it had failed miserably.

"Friendly enough if he knocked on the door and declared he was ready to march in Pride parades, you'd fall right back in with him?" Brock asked, a challenging gleam in his eyes.

Before this job?

Yeah, maybe.

Before the heat between Brock and me sparked back to life, his solid frame against mine, his taste on my tongue?

Possibly.

Now?

No way.

I shook my head. "Nah, Aaron and I weren't a good fit. I realize that now." I took a drink of beer. "What about you? Got a boyfriend back in town? Husband?"

Brock shook his head, a twinkle in his eyes. "No. Been busy lately—which is good—doesn't leave a lot of time for dating."

"Guess it's a good thing Bernard showed up." I gestured toward the TV. "Work by day, shitty-reception news dates by night," I teased.

Brock chuckled. "Yeah, show me a good time, baby," he shot back, grinning.

We fiddled with the television, converter, and

antenna for a bit, finally getting a somewhat fuzzy channel to come through. After watching the top stories and the weather, I switched off the set.

"Well, that's about all I need of that," I said.

"Nice of Bernard, but it's definitely not my flat-screen and streaming service." Brock gathered up our trash and threw it away while I wiped off the table.

As we made our way around the house, doing a nightly check as we'd made a habit of doing, I almost wondered if I'd imagined those kisses from earlier in the day.

Were we going to ignore the spark?

Was Bernard's interruption a nail in the coffin?

Was Brock not interested?

Or was I just making way too much of things?

I checked through some emails while Brock took a quick shower.

"You wanna maybe check out the basement at some point?" he called from the bathroom. "The room Bernard talked about?"

"Do I want to go back down in that creepy basement, find a secret room where a mortician kept bodies, and look for a mysterious box that may or may not give insight into our very own ghost?" I deadpanned back.

He stuck his head around the corner of the bathroom door with a grin. "Yeah?"

Momentarily distracted by his wet hair and water droplets glistening in the smattering of hair on his chest, I eventually pulled my attention from the enticing treasure trail leading under the towel wrapped around his waist and focused on his question as he ducked back into the bathroom. "Doesn't sound like my favorite way to spend time," a brief image of Brock on his knees for me flashed through my head, "but it may be helpful. Just know, basements creep me out. The thought of a secret room sounds doubly creepy."

Brock chuckled as he walked out of the bathroom in only a loose pair of lounge pants and hung his damp towel over the arm of the couch. "I left you some water. Crimson needs to think about increasing the size of the tank here if he wants hot water to last longer than five minutes."

Wanting to spend money to stay at a haunted house seemed strange to me, but I guessed there would be people who definitely wanted to do it, and they'd probably want hot showers.

I smiled as I shucked off my clothes and stepped under the spray. Our ghost wasn't at all scary—okay, that wasn't accurate, he was spooky until you got used to him, but he'd never done anything truly scary. Kinda a friendly ghost. Thinking about how long he'd been here—likely alone, probably sad, maybe struggling with getting to the other side—sent a pang through my chest.

Brock's laughter from the other room pulled me from my thoughts as I lathered soap in all the most important locations and scrubbed sawdust from my hair.

My dick immediately jumped to attention at the

thought of Brock—ridiculously, I wanted to know what he was laughing at, what he enjoyed, what made him tick—and my mind replayed the earlier kisses and the sloppy, awkward blowjobs from way back when.

As the water rained down on me, rinsing away the long day's work under the soap bubbles, I stroked my cock. If Brock was going to pretend like we hadn't had a moment back in the kitchen, maybe I could rub one out before the water ran cold.

As if my thoughts were a switch, the shower spray turned icy cold and I yelped. Dropping my dick, which lost interest the moment an Arctic blast rendered it useless, I stepped away from the gush of cold water and glanced at the old-fashioned knobs.

"You okay? What happened?" Brock asked from outside the curtain.

I reached out and grabbed my towel, wrapping it around my waist before yanking open the curtain, exiting the shower, and pointing at the knobs.

"What do you see there?" I demanded.

Brock's eyes roamed up and down my wet chest for several seconds before tearing from me and looking at the knobs. "You turned the hot all the way off and left the cold running?" He eyed me as if it were a trick question.

"*I* didn't do anything," I bit out. "Water went ice cold, I didn't touch those knobs."

Brock's brow shot up. "Ghosty?" he asked to the room. "You playing tricks on my friend here? Bad ghost, bad." He smirked my way. "You piss him off?"

I shrugged, cold droplets falling from my wet hair to my shoulders. "Maybe he's just playing games? We know he's kinda a pain. Or he didn't like the talk of us searching the secret room?"

Or he didn't want you jacking off if there's a chance you and Brock might get down and dirty...

The thought hit me like a ton of bricks.

Shit.

First, it kinda creeped me out to think the spirit was watching me. I wasn't against a partner watching me get myself off, but the idea of a one-hundred-year-old ghost watching me stroke my cock was a bit unnerving.

Second, why was he so insistent Brock and I get together? Not that I was complaining. If ghosty wanted to assist in getting me laid, I was all for it. Just wasn't sure about the *why* behind it. Just a lonely, horny ghost?

Third, maybe our ghost had a point. Getting off with Brock was a lot more enticing than a lonely jerk-off in a lukewarm shower.

But would Brock even be interested?

I thought back to the press of his bulge against mine in the kitchen.

Maybe I'd ruined chances for an actual relationship when I ran off all those years ago, but Brock's body against mine had definitely shown interest in at least something physical.

But if I let a physical relationship develop, was I any better than that kid way back then who let Brock suck me off—nearly begged for it, in fact—and then ran away?

Brock reached out to turn off the cold water knob. "He's pretty skilled. Guess he's had plenty of time to figure out his tricks." He glanced at me and I swore the hunger in his eyes was real. Swallowing, his Adam's apple bobbing, Brock dipped his head and made for the door. "Sorry you got iced," he mumbled as he left me alone in the tiny bathroom.

Okay, that was definitely interest.

Right?

I yanked on a pair of boxers, rubbed the excess water from my hair, and hung my towel on the back of the door before heading into the bedroom.

The space was really nice and would have likely been considered luxurious when it was first built. I wondered if this was the room where the mother died during childbirth. Was she our ghost? Or was it her baby haunting the place? Her husband?

Maybe getting some answers would help shed some light on our resident haunter. Would delving into the mysteries of the past allow the spirit to eventually find peace? Were his pushes to get Brock and I together part of him finding peace?

I crawled into bed, the room mostly dark except for the bit of moonlight shining through the open windows. Brock had put his phone on the charger, but I could tell from his breathing he wasn't asleep.

"Maybe this ghost thing has me all fucked up, but..." I hedged.

Brock rolled to face me, a large amount of space between our bodies. "Yeah?"

"Did I imagine something in the kitchen earlier?" I asked.

He huffed out a breath. "If you were imagining, I was having the same thoughts."

"You got any thoughts on it?" I wanted to reach for him, draw him close, breathe him in, and savor every inch of him.

"About a million and none of them doing me much good," Brock answered gruffly.

"Care to share?"

"I know it was years ago, but the kid I used to be was crushed when you left. I *knew* you weren't out and maybe never would be, but that never stopped my fantasies." He shifted, bringing our bodies a fraction of an inch closer together. "I wasn't joking about the fact I've been thinking about bringing on a partner in the business. We work well together. What if we fall into bed and fuck shit up as far as working together? What if we keep things platonic and miss out on shit we lost when you left?" He paused. "What about you? Thoughts?"

"Honestly, part of me wants to be a total man, ignore thoughts and feelings, fuck you senseless, and let what happens happen," I admitted.

"And the other part?" Brock asked, a smile in his words.

"That part has the same thoughts you do. I want you, never stopped wanting you. But we work well together and I don't want to fuck that up. Not pinning my hopes on the business thing just yet, but it sounds real good. Do we risk losing that?"

We fell silent for a few moments.

"Do you remember the other day when you asked me why I told you the truth about me and I said it was because I owed it to the kid I used to be?" I asked.

Brock took a heartbeat to answer. "Yeah?"

"Well," I cleared my throat, "maybe I also owed it to the kid you used to be. I wasn't fair to you and that's eaten at me all this time. You deserved better than what I could give back then."

He made a noncommittal noise. "We were kids. We didn't have much of anything to give." After a moment, he spoke again, his words soft and gruff. "Is that all this has been? Making amends to the kids we used to be?"

I let the question sit briefly. "Maybe I also feel like I owe it to the men we are now? Owe us a chance? Maybe it's just good sex? Maybe it ends up being more? I'm not dead set on finding my forever, but I'm also at a point where I'm not looking for random, meaningless hookups."

Brock's next words were gravelly and close enough I could feel his breath on my face. "Speaking of the kids we used to be, do you know how much I used to get off thinking about sucking your cock?"

Said cock shot from plump and hopeful to steely and throbbing in half a second. "Probably as much as I got off thinking about your lips around me." Images from the past mixed with the thick sexual tension swirling between us. "You still give head as good as back then?"

Brock snorted. "Like to think I've improved over the years. Wanna find out?"

"Fuck yes," I moaned. "But first..." Reaching out a hand, I gripped the back of his neck and pulled him close. "Never got enough of kissing you. Always hiding, rushing, too concerned about getting my dick out."

"Pretty sure both our dicks would be happy to skip the kissing," Brock said, a smile playing on his words as he rolled his rock-hard cock against mine.

"You got a thing against kissing?" While our earlier kisses in the kitchen suggested he was completely on board, I knew some people skipped kissing, claiming it was too intimate. But I wanted that intimacy with him. Wanted to hold him close, devour his mouth, taste him on my tongue.

Brock's lips feathered over mine. "Not at all."

With a groan, I closed the distance and captured his mouth. He tasted of mint and man, of long-ago memories and future possibilities, and I wanted to savor him forever. Soft warm lips, slick delving tongues, and hands gripping hair carried me away to fantasies I hadn't known I still held onto.

"Since laundry is an issue," I said when I broke the kiss, panting, "I'd rather not ruin these clothes. You comfortable with getting naked?"

Brock just grunted and yanked his pants down and I all but ripped off my boxers. Our clothing found its way to the floor and our hard, hot bodies came together like opposite poles on a magnet.

We'd never been completely naked together.

I'd never had the opportunity to feel him plastered against me, no rush, no secrecy. Never had the chance to let my hands roam over his glorious body, loving every hard plane, angle, and curve of muscle. I palmed his ass and pulled him close, thrusting our leaking cocks together.

"What do you want?" I growled.

"Fuck," Brock grunted. "Everything."

"At the risk of losing out on *everything*, let's take it slow." As much as I wanted to slide my dick in his ass, I also wanted to enjoy the fact we could take our time. My hand reached between our rocking hips and gripped his length. "Wanna suck you."

Brock's only answer was to thrust into my fist.

Memories of him on his knees for me—back when I thought I didn't have to think about being gay as long as guys were sucking me off and not the other way around—spurred me to roll from the bed and stand. "Sit on the edge," I ordered.

When Brock moved to the side of the bed, his long legs hanging over the edge, cock bobbing enticingly against his abs, I stepped between his thighs, tipped his chin up, and smothered his mouth in a searing kiss.

Loving the glazed longing in his eyes as he watched me, I dropped to my knees. "Back then, I couldn't admit how badly I wanted this." Fondling his balls, I licked the tip of his cockhead, savoring the bitter saltiness of pre-cum before taking him deep. I loved the heavy weight of his hot, silky cock on my tongue, the stretch of my lips around his width, and the press of his tip teasing the back of my throat.

"Fuck, Calder. Fucking hell," Brock groaned.

I would have happily sucked him to completion, but after a few moments, Brock pulled back and hauled me to the mattress. He kissed me slow and deep, grunting against my lips as his flavor danced between our tongues.

Brock quickly shifted our bodies into a sideways sixty-nine position and I greedily took his cock back between my lips before my fingers traveled to his ass and brushed over his sensitive hole.

The wet heat engulfing my shaft had me bucking my hips and groaning around Brock's cock.

Holy.

Fucking.

Shit.

Brock Shelton gave good head way back then.

Either he'd had a lot of practice since or I'd been getting a lot of inferior blow jobs—maybe a combination of both—but, holy hell, the man sucked me like a damn pro.

When his wet finger pressed against my entrance, my balls tightened and I knew I wasn't going to last much longer.

"Wanna taste you in my throat, feel you unload on my tongue, and grip my fingers," Brock gasped the words when he popped off my cock.

"Fuck, yes. Give 'em to me."

"You have lube?" Brock asked.

"In my bag," I panted. "Don't wanna stop."

"Don't wanna hurt you," Brock protested.

Something hard and cold hit my back and I jerked. "What the hell?"

Brock laughed as he reached for whatever had hit me. "Thanks, Ghosty, but maybe you could give us some privacy?"

The door swung shut with a click.

"Fuck," I groaned, my dick still throbbing. "Is it bad I don't even care if he watches? I just wanna feel you come."

We took a moment to coat our fingers before returning to gorging ourselves on each other's cocks. Brock's slick fingers slid over my hole, teasing and taunting until he finally pressed his way in and quickly added a second digit when I pleaded for more.

I returned the favor, groaning when his tight heat opened for me, imagining how good his ass would feel around my cock.

We settled into a satisfying rhythm of sucking and fingering, slick fingers pumping, greedy tongues swirling, and rock-hard cocks thrusting. The air was warm from the fire, thick with the scent of sex, and our grunts and groans danced through the otherwise silent house.

If our ghost was watching, he was getting a show.

Hell, even if he was only listening, he was getting a show.

When Brock's fingers brushed over that bundle of nerves deep inside, I hummed around his shaft. Our pace increased and all-too-soon we were both grunting through our releases, swallowing thick spurts of cum against the back of our throats, and riding out our pleasure.

Between the hard work we'd been putting in, the orgasms, and the mysteries of the house, Brock and I were both ready to crash. We took a moment to wipe up, cuddled back in bed, and fell into a deep, satisfied sleep. Any concerns or regrets could be addressed in the morning.

five
brock

As TORN as my head and heart wanted to be over letting things go that far with Calder, I couldn't help the warm, cuddly, satisfied feeling washing over me when I woke a bit later curled in his arms.

Yeah, we had a bit of a sordid past.

Yeah, he'd walked away.

Yeah, we were working together.

Yeah, we'd talked about making the work thing more permanent.

Yeah, sleeping with him could bring an avalanche of bad shit down on us.

In all honesty, I couldn't even bring myself to care.

Our past was just that, the past.

We'd been young and dumb.

Did it hurt when I had to admit he was using me and was nowhere close to ready to come out?

Yes.

Was it doubly painful when I realized he'd left town, likely to get away from me?

Yes, definitely.

Could getting involved with Calder again possibly mess things up?

Yes. I wasn't going into the situation lying to myself.

But his arms around me, his lips on mine, his cock on my tongue...

Fuck.

All of those things—hell, even just laughing with him, working side-by-side, getting to know him all over again...as grown men and not clueless teens—all of it nearly brought me to my knees.

How many years had I been dreaming of having this with Calder?

Correction.

Dreaming of having *this* with anyone.

But having Calder be the man I was getting that chance with reminded me just how much of a thing I'd had for him back then.

True, as a teen, I'd basically just been horny and thought he was hot. As bad as it sounds, I didn't really care whose cock I was worshipping as long as it was in my mouth and coming down my throat.

But now...well, now I'd been given a chance to get to know Calder as a person.

Yes, he was still drop-dead gorgeous.

Yes, gagging on his dick was still top on my list of favorite things to do.

Yes, his kisses still set me on fire.

But there was more to it than that.

And despite knowing I maybe should have regretted what we'd done or have concerns about what might come next, I just couldn't bring myself to be too terribly upset.

Calder shifted and mumbled something in his sleep. With my ass tucked against his cock, I couldn't help but squirm slightly and rock back into him.

I knew the moment he woke.

The room was still bathed in darkness, and I guessed we had about four hours before our alarms would sound. Plenty of time for a second round and a bit more sleep before our day began.

Calder's thick, hard shaft pressed against my ass. His lips nuzzled my neck. His hand caressed my shoulder, my torso, and my hip. "You need somethin'?" he whispered gruffly against my ear.

"Make me come," I demanded, sounding a bit more desperate than intended.

As badly as I wanted him inside me, things felt a bit too new between us for that just yet. I had condoms. We had lube. I'd gladly bottom for him—with or without the condom if the conversation came up and we agreed. But we had a lot of time to make up for and I was in no hurry.

Calder reached for the bottle of lube, slicked himself, and thrust his cock between my thighs. We groaned in unison as his shaft pressed against my balls. "Keep your legs tight together," he commanded, taking my leaking, throbbing cock in his fist and stroking me.

Calder set a slow and easy pace, fucking between my legs, his shaft caressing my taint and balls as he jerked me off. "Fucking hell, you're so damn good," he growled. "Can't wait to be in that sexy ass of yours, filling you with my cum."

My rocking hips faltered at the image he painted for me.

His next words took me by surprise, but were no less of a turn-on. "Gonna bend over and take this pretty cock too. Wanna feel you stretch me open, feel my ass grip your fat cock."

Calder being vers wasn't something I'd ever thought about.

In the past, it was me sucking him off.

Me stroking us to completion.

The sexual encounters we'd had were sloppy and brief. Nothing back then had made me think he'd want to bottom.

"Wanna feel your cum dripping from my ass," he continued, his words low and dirty.

With images of him fucking me and me fucking him dancing through my head, I increased the thrusting of my hips and groaned as my balls drew up tight. "Fuck, Calder, gonna come."

"Fuck, come with me," Calder demanded.

In the next moment, a hot, wet sensation painted my balls and my release shot over Calder's fist. Riding out our orgasms, reveling in the grunts and heavy breathing, sinking into his strong arms around me, I realized I was falling way too fast and way too deep.

There wasn't a thing I could do about it.

Even if I wanted to.

And I was pretty sure I didn't want to.

"Let's shower now. We can sleep thirty minutes longer and not have to shower in the morning," Calder said.

"It *is* morning," I grumped as we rolled from bed.

Calder slapped my ass and chuckled. "All the more reason to clean up and get some extra sleep. We've got two fairly large projects to work on tomorrow."

"And a secret room to explore."

Calder shivered. "Don't remind me."

After a quick shower, we curled together in bed, and slept like babies until our early morning wake-up call.

"You wanna plan a laundry run sometime soon?" I asked Calder as we took a final moment to enjoy our coffee before starting our work for the day.

I'd woken feeling out of sorts, but it hadn't had anything to do with the man in my bed. The last little jag of sleep I'd gotten had been fitful, and Calder had seemed plagued by the same.

"Calder?" I asked again, turning from my phone to see what was keeping him from answering me.

He was gone.

What the hell?

I stalked to the kitchen sink and looked out the window to the backyard.

That unsettled feeling washed over me again and I rushed from the backdoor and down the rickety old steps.

When I reached Calder, standing under a large oak tree, a dream I hadn't remembered came rushing back.

"I dreamed about this tree," Calder mumbled, his hand reaching out to trace the heart carved in the wood.

Images from the dream flashed through my head. The swing, the heart, the initials, and something terrifying clutched at my heart. There was a mixture of emotions swirling through my chest. Happiness and love, but the images kept going dark and dangerous. Fear and pain coursed through me.

"So did I," I whispered.

"They were in love." Calder's fingers caressed the outline of the heart and the letters P and C inside the crudely carved shape. "And very scared."

I took Calder's free hand and squeezed.

He broke from whatever trance the images in his head had him in.

Pointing to another carved area of the tree, I spoke softly, unsure of why we'd had the same dream about this tree. "P hearts Ren."

Calder frowned. "Why P and C in the heart and P hearts Ren over on this side?"

"P fell in love with two people?"

Calder shook his head. "That's not the feeling I'm

getting. The dream—I didn't even remember it until I glanced out and saw the tree—the dream made it very clear P was head-over-heels in love. Like a once-in-a-lifetime love. I don't think P carved two different initials."

"Maybe P isn't the same person? Maybe we're seeing two different couples here?"

"I don't know. I just know that the P in my dream was happily in love and then terrified for his life." Calder tugged me close, never dropping my hand. "You feel any breeze right now?" he asked quietly.

"Not at all. Still as can be. Why?"

"The swing."

I glanced toward the old-fashioned swing, the hairs on the back of my neck standing up. It moved as if a person was sitting on it, pumping his legs or being pushed from behind, but there wasn't a person on the swing.

And there wasn't a single hint of a breeze.

"You think our ghost is P?" I asked.

"Makes sense. But I don't feel like we can jump to conclusions." Calder turned toward me, tipped my chin, and brushed a kiss over my lips. "Maybe he's stuck here because of whatever was terrifying him? I don't pretend to understand anything about spirits or whatever, but if he needs us to figure something out, I'll gladly set aside my fears and help him escape." A tremor shuddered through him as he hugged me close.

"You okay?" I asked.

"Just thinking about how scared he felt in that

dream. Scared and so sad. Like he'd lost something and blamed himself." Calder pressed his forehead against mine. "If P is our ghost—I know we have to get some better clues for accuracy—but if he's our ghost, he's likely been stuck here for about one hundred years. Sad, lonely, maybe still scared? Whoever C or Ren is, did he lose them? Has he been trying to get to them all this time?" He shook his head. "I don't get why we seem to be the ones he chose to help him—hell, maybe we're the only ones who haven't chickened out and run away or we're just the first to take time and pay enough attention to know he's in need—but I'm not running from this and I'm not leaving him to suffer."

I captured his mouth in a kiss. "I really like the man you've become. You're one of the good ones, Calder Mills."

He broke from the kiss, his eyes boring into mine as if he wanted to say something, but he just kissed me once more and turned toward the house. "We've got work to do if we're going to explore that secret room."

Our day passed easily as we finished a project, completed a second one, and started a third one. By the time we called it a day, we were exhausted and hungry. The light lunch we'd scarfed down at noon was long forgotten.

"Let's do soup and bread for dinner. Can use the rest of that lunchmeat before it goes bad. We need to run into town to get groceries and do laundry," I suggested.

Throughout the entire day, our ghost—who we

now thought of as P—slammed doors, ruffled curtains, opened and shut windows, and unplugged our tools.

As we started to cook dinner, the lights went off and Calder huffed. "Look," he said to the room as he flipped the lights back on, "we get it. You're here. You're scared maybe. You need something. We want to help and we're going to do what we can, but can you at least let us eat first?"

The strike of a match caught our attention as a candle flamed to life. A soft calm fell over the room as if P was letting us know he was willing to be patient.

Calder gave me a nod and we went about fixing our meal, eating, and chatting. We'd fallen into such a comfortable routine over the month and then some we'd been working and I didn't want to give a single moment to thinking about when we were no longer in a forced proximity situation.

Would Calder decide it was best if he struck out on his own?

Would what we had in the haunted mansion crumble when we were back in the real world, faced with business and interpersonal challenges?

Would he run again?

Calder reached for my hand. "You're thinking pretty loudly over there."

"Just wanna help him," I said, ignoring where my head had really gone. "Can't imagine being stuck here all this time." I glanced around the kitchen. "So lonely…"

"We'll figure it out. Come on, let's finish and head to the basement."

"You look like you'd rather stab forks into your eyes," I teased.

"Well…" Calder huffed. "Basements are usually creepy and we *know* this one isn't super cheery. A secret room, the fact this place housed a lot of dead bodies throughout several years, and the unknown has me completely freaked out. I'm man enough to be able to admit that."

As we washed and dried our dishes, possibly moving a bit slowly to stall the inevitable trip to the basement, a clicking noise sounded from the kitchen table and the old television set came to life.

Calder and I turned to face the TV, arms brushing as the knobs clicked and the picture faded in and out.

"Are you seeing this?" Calder whispered.

"Yep," I answered.

Standing in complete silent awe, we watched as a black and white news broadcast came into focus on the screen.

"Good evening, tonight we'd like to bring you a public interest story. This is the third in our series of stories focusing on the mysterious happenings in our state. This time, we travel to Prairie Brook and the home of Mr. Presley Wade King. Mr. King was, by all accounts, an odd duck. But he met and married Miss Sonya Linds in 1897. King built a home in Prairie Brook meant to be filled with happiness, children, and love in 1898. Sonya King became pregnant with the couple's first child, but sadly died in childbirth in 1900. The baby, a Presley Allen King, grew up as the only child of the senior King."

The broadcaster turned to his counterpart. "Jim, this is likely the saddest of our series if I'm being honest."

"You're right, Don. Not a lot of happiness followed this family. The senior King was a mortician—from what our reporter could gather, he'd planned the house to be a funeral home, but it was just too far outside of town. So, he set up a mortuary business, took care of bodies, and delivered them to churches and funeral homes nearby. It's said Mr. King was a unique individual and never recovered after losing his wife. Reports state he kept to himself and collected oddities in addition to caring for the deceased. Unfortunately, at age eighteen, his son found Mr. King dead of self-inflicted wounds. It's said the senior King hanged himself. Very little is known about Presley King, Junior other than he sold off most of his father's business belongings, kept the house, and four years later, in 1922, was found dead of suspected murder. Several rumors about the younger King circulated around his death, including suspicions about the boarder who was also found dead with Presley, Junior." Jim paused and turned to Don for the rest of the story.

"Unlike some of the other stories in this series, we don't have a lot of answers regarding the mysteries surrounding the King home and family. The house remains untouched in Prairie Brook even now, fifty years after the younger King was found dead. Were King and his boarder murdered as rumors indicate? Was there more to the two men than boarder and homeowner as some of the more salacious stories would have us believe? Is the home haunted by ghosts from years and years of death surrounding the family and structure?" Don looked straight at the camera. "Jim, there are still a lot of questions that may never be answered."

The television set went black, smoke trailing from the back as the scent of melted wiring filled the air.

"What the actual fuck just happened?" Calder mumbled.

"If the younger Presley died in 1922, and that news story was on the fifty-year anniversary of his death, we just watched something from 1972." I ran my hand through my hair.

"But we've got a couple answers now. Maybe." Calder huffed. "And probably even more questions."

"Do we even want to try to figure out how a 1972 news story found its way to our old junker TV set when we didn't even have it turned on?" I mused.

"Based on the smoke, I'd say no. I'm guessing our spirit—or whatever paranormal forces are at work in this house—made that happen and it's best to just not question," Calder answered gruffly.

"Should we head to the basement?"

six
calder

ARMED WITH A FLASHLIGHT I wielded like a baseball bat, my phone, and a pair of work gloves stuffed in my back pocket, I followed Brock down the steps to the basement. "Shit, this place was creepy the first time we came down here and it hasn't gotten better."

Brock paused at the bottom of the stairs and shone his own flashlight around.

The space wasn't anything close to a finished basement.

More like a cellar if I was being honest.

The floors were packed dirt, the walls stopped halfway up, and then a sort of in-set shelf or ledge continued around the entire room. Three tiny, dingy windows let in the very last hints of light as the sun sank beyond the horizon.

"How did he get bodies down here? No way he took them up and down these steps," Brock mumbled.

"Shhh, do you hear that?" The hairs on the back of

my neck stood up as the air filled with hints of whispers and soft sobbing.

"Fuck, yeah. Are we assuming P is Presley?" Brock asked, referring to the news story and what little information we'd gathered from the initials on the tree.

"Yeah, but which one? The older or younger?"

Brock shrugged. "You think that's him whispering and crying?"

An icy cold wave washed over me.

"No. I think Presley just joined us." I glanced around the dim, shadowy basement. "Maybe there are other ghosts down here? Spirits? I don't know, but this is freakin' me the fuck out. Let's find this damn secret room, look for the box, and get out of here."

Brock took the last step to the dirt floor and swung his flashlight around. "I don't like that chest freezer being plugged in down here if it doesn't have to be. It's pulling power and it's a fire hazard with that frayed cord. Hell, doubt it's even keeping anything cold. I say we check to be sure there's nothing in it and unplug it."

I nearly plastered myself to his back as he headed toward the freezer, both of us needing to duck slightly so as to keep our heads from brushing against the floor beams of the ceiling overhead. "It had been unplugged for who-knows-how-long before we flipped that breaker. I say we unplug it and leave it alone."

Brock chuckled and turned to face me, wrapped his arms around me, and pressed a kiss to my lips. "You're kinda cute when you're scared."

I huffed and deepened the kiss for a moment before

the whispers and sobs got too distracting. "You can't tell me it's not freaky as fuck down here. It's dark, cold, there are sounds that shouldn't be here, and we're looking for a hidden room. Check your freezer and let's get on with it."

Brock smacked a kiss to my lips and turned back toward the freezer. "I'm guessing it's mostly just gonna be terribly rancid more than anything." He pointed his light at the lid and slowly lifted it.

When he jumped and fell backwards with a yelp, I jerked and grunted, moving away from the freezer to help him up. "What's in there?"

Brock snorted. "God, this sounds like that movie. *What's in the box?*" He gestured toward the freezer. "Um, I'm not completely sure, but I swear I saw faces."

"Faces? What the fuck?" With more bravery than I was really feeling, I yanked him to stand and made my way toward the freezer. Peering over the edge, I gave my own yelp of fear and stepped away. "Fuck no. I'm not dealing with this shit. Why are there faces in the freezer?"

Brock took a deep breath and moved closer to take another peek. "Oh my god. They're dolls. Like those dummy dolls—the kind ventriloquists use. Seriously, they aren't real. Just dolls. Come see." He held a hand out to me.

"I'll just take your word for it." I shook my head, my chest seizing as I recalled those faces staring up at me.

"No, you need to see it so you can breathe again." Brock pulled me closer.

"No one *ever* needs to see a bunch of eyes staring at him from an old freezer." But I let him shift me to the edge of the old freezer and I glanced in again. "God, that's the creepiest thing I've ever seen. Why are they all just staring? Who thought making these stupid dolls was a good idea?"

"And why are they here? *In a freezer?* There are so many questions."

"Well, that news story said Mr. Presley, Senior was an odd duck." I shivered. I would *never* forget those glassy eyes staring up at me.

"Yep, this fits odd. Okay, let's unplug it. Once we figure out how he got the bodies in and out of here, we'll see about getting the freezer out. It's not at all cold so it's definitely not working. No need to keep it down here." Brock reached down and yanked the old cord from the wall.

I finally stopped clutching my flashlight like a weapon and turned it on.

Together, Brock and I shone our lights over the walls.

"There," I said, pointing toward a door blending into the far wall. "That must be our secret room."

"You think it's locked?"

The door swung open as an icy cold sensation washed over me.

"Thanks, Presley," Brock ventured as he took my hand. "Come on. Let's get this over with."

The sounds of sobbing and whispering grew louder with the door open.

"Who the hell is down here?" I whispered frantically. "Why are they down here? Are they stuck?" The sobs and whispers were making me panic and I wanted to cover my ears.

"They need to be told to go to the beyond."

The voice was soft and scratchy, but I knew immediately it was Presley.

"What?" Brock asked me.

"It wasn't me. It was Presley. He says the spirits need to be told to go on to the beyond." I gestured toward the sobs and whispers.

"That's all it takes?"

I shrugged.

Brock shone his flashlight around the secret room and jumped with a howl.

I pointed my light in the same direction and cursed. "What the fuck? How many of those damn things does he have?" A three-shelf built-in covered the farthest wall of the tiny room and about ten ventriloquist dolls sat on the shelves, their eyes staring right at us, their mouths in a variety of opened and closed positions. "Those fuckers have always freaked me out and now I'll *never* be able to see them without nearly shitting my pants."

Brock chuckled. "I wonder if they're worth any money. I bet we could get an antique dealer down here and make some cash."

"Or Bernard could."

"True. For some reason, this place feels like so much more than just a project. Like we belong here." Brock gestured toward another door. "Maybe this is his hobby room and *that* is the secret room."

As another icy breeze filled the room, the door swung open, the hinges creaking.

Our flashlights lit up the room filled with three old medical-type cots, counters where I could imagine mortuary supplies being stored, and another door.

As the whispers and sobs filled the room, I pointed toward the third door. "Wanna bet that goes outside? I'm guessing that's where he brought the bodies to and from his work area."

Brock and I yanked on the door and it opened with a whoosh.

"Oh my god. A creepy basement and damn freaky dolls aren't bad enough? Now I've got to deal with spiders?" I shuddered.

Brock laughed. "Okay, as much as I'd rather blow-torch them, I think we can knock them down and open that door." He grabbed a broom and brushed it through the spider webs covering the little hallway to the last door and I refused to think about how that was just disturbing the bastards instead of killing every single one of them the way I wanted to.

"Why do we need to open it? Let's just look for the box."

"I think we need to see where it goes and also maybe the open door will allow the crying spirits to leave."

I sighed. "Okay, fine. Go open it."

Brock rolled his eyes. "You just going to wait there for me while I travel into danger?"

"It's just a little dirt path through spiders," I say, knowing how pathetic I sounded.

Brock batted his lashes at me and I huffed.

"Fine. Let's go."

He took my hand and we rushed through the little slanted hallway. I pretended I didn't feel any webs or spiders on my head, face, and hands.

"Here it is," Brock said and he slammed himself against a wooden door.

When we finally got it open, it was easy to see we were in the yard at the side of the house.

"Okay, let's go back and tell them they can leave," Brock said.

We made our way back through the tunnel.

"What do we say to them?" I asked.

"Just tell them they are free to leave, they are no longer needed here, they can go to the beyond."

Presley's words filled the air, barely audible over the whispers and sobs.

Brock cleared his throat. "I'm not feeling very sure about this," he mumbled.

"Give it a shot. If it doesn't work, we'll grab the box, go upstairs, and never come down here again."

"And if it works?"

I shrugged. "We'll grab the box and never come down here again."

"Spirits of the house," Brock started, "you are free to

leave this place. You're no longer needed here. You can go to the beyond."

For a moment, the sobs and whispers continued and I was sure it hadn't worked.

And then...

The sobs and whispers traveled across the room, an icy sensation kissing over my skin, and the sounds disappeared through the tunnel.

Brock grabbed my hand, raced to the outer door, slammed it shut, ran through the inner door, frantically closing it behind us, and rushed us back to the clinic room.

"Oh my god, did we just free spirits?" he asked, breathing heavily.

"I think so. I'm not thinking we're the next ghostbusters, but I think we helped them at least." I shone my light around the room. "And now I'm beyond freaked out so let's get this box and get upstairs."

A rustling noise to our right made us both jump and we turned our lights to see a box being pushed across the counter.

"Okay, thanks to Presley, I think we've found our box." I grabbed the wooden box. It reminded me of an apple crate, but it had a lid and no spaces between the wooden slats.

Brock and I basically ran up the stairs and slammed the door shut.

"Let's fix some tea, take showers, and settle in with the box in front of the fire," Brock suggested.

When the candle was blown out, I knew Presley was getting impatient.

"Pres, I swear, we're going to help you. We've been working all day. Let us shower and settle in, then the rest of the night is devoted to figuring out your story. Promise," I said.

"He's anxious," Brock said.

"Yeah, seems like it. This may be the closest anyone has ever gotten to learning his story and helping him escape." I put a kettle of water on the stove to boil. "You shower, I'll fix the tea."

Twenty minutes later, we were both at least clean, if not relaxed, from quick showers, and we carried steaming mugs of tea into the bedroom, shut the door, and settled in front of the fire Brock had started.

"I wonder why we can't just tell Presley he's free to leave," Brock mused, sipping his tea, his back against the couch, legs stretched out toward the fire.

The box was between us and the fire and lamps gave us just enough light to see.

"Maybe he's stuck here for a different reason," I said.

A chill washed over the room.

"*They were inadvertently caught here. Some spirits need a little push to cross over. My father would speak to them. When he died, he left without giving them permission to go to the beyond. At the time, I didn't know I could have sent them on their way.*"

"And you're here for a different reason?" I asked in

the direction Presley's voice had come from. "Oh! You're the Presley King, Junior then?"

"Yes, this was my father's house before it was mine. I'm here as punishment, but I need to cross over. It's been one hundred years since my death and I'm desperate to join my love."

"Do you want us to look in this box?" Brock asked, glancing around the room as if trying to figure out where Presley was. "Or would you rather just tell us your story?"

"Speaking takes a lot out of me. I only figured out how to do it recently. Please, look in the box. I'll do my best to fill in holes and answer questions."

"Can we see you?" I asked.

"Perhaps, but not yet. I'm working on it."

Brock lifted the lid of the box and whistled. "This is like a box of sex toys for a historian."

"Do historians like sex toys?" I teased.

"You know what I mean. It's a box of historical treasure. The right person would totally get off on this."

"I'd rather we just get some answers. We can get off later," I whispered gruffly in his ear.

"Awww, such a sweet talker." Brock pulled out a bundle of photographs and a leather-bound book. "Pictures first?" he asked.

"I'm in. We're getting closer, Presley. Just you wait. Soon, you'll be heading off to your very own great beyond."

"Halloween."

"Halloween? Why Halloween?" Brock cocked his head. "That's just over three weeks from now."

"What's special about Halloween?" I asked.

"Let him save his voice," Brock answered. "Pictures first, then the notebook."

THE STACK of photographs held a musty scent.

I kept my fingers on the scalloped edges of the relics, knowing oils from my hands would mark up the prints. Holding something so old was a surreal feeling.

"The very first photographs were in 1826," Calder mused as he read from a Google page on his phone. "Check these for dates. I bet names and dates were written on some."

I spread out the images in what seemed to be chronological order based on the state of the paper. Then we began carefully picking up each print and checking the back for dates and names.

A few were so old and crumbly, we couldn't even tell what had been in the picture. A handful didn't have anything written on the back. But we hit the jackpot with a set of three photos with curly, scrawled handwriting on the back.

Sonya Linds and Presley Wade King, 1896.

"These are Presley's parents," I murmured.

Presley, Senior was a gangly man with somewhat wild hair, a grim smile, and prominent ears.

Sonya was smaller in stature, hair swept up in what would have surely been the style at that time, and a soft, simple smile.

The next photograph appeared to be of their wedding.

Mr. and Mrs. Presley Wade King, 1897.

While it was evident the image was from their wedding, the bride and groom appeared to be in very simple wedding attire which led me to believe the Kings weren't super affluent. Or all of his money had been saved for building the house a year later.

The third picture, dated 1898 was of Sonya and Presley, Senior in front of the very home we were sitting in. The surreal wave of the situation wafted over me once again.

The senior King, still gawky and grim—although, sporting a fairly proud smile—seemed quite pleased with the home he'd built for his bride. Mrs. King beamed as if she'd just been given the world.

And if their plan was to fill the home with love and family, they had every right to look so happy and excited. I hated that things would fall apart for them so soon. They had such plans for their future—or I assumed they did—and despair was right around the corner. They had no clue.

The last photograph we found of Sonya was dated 1899.

"There are no leaves on the trees, so this must have been late in that year," Calder mused.

"Look at you, my super sleuth," I teased, leaning in close, loving the warmth of his body pressed against my side. "But yeah, you're right."

"From what you said, and from the news story, we know Presley, Junior was born in 1900. If she died during childbirth, she's possibly already pregnant in this picture or will be soon after."

We peered at the photograph, trying to decipher if her waistline looked bigger than in other pictures.

All I knew for sure was that Sonya's face disappeared from the photos as we continued to sift through them.

There were no baby pictures of the younger Presley.

"His father must have been distraught," I murmured.

"Father never recovered from the loss."

"I'm sorry," I said to our ghost. "I'm sorry for his loss and for yours."

"More his than mine. He'd loved her, I never even knew her."

The first photograph of Presley we came across was a school class picture dated 1912. From that date on, there was a school picture each year.

Until 1918 when he would have presumably graduated.

No photographs of father and son together.

A photograph of two men dated 1920 was the last one in the pile.

"Is this you?" Calder asked Presley, even though we couldn't see him and it felt slightly strange to be talking to an empty room.

"Yes. The diary will be more helpful."

I studied the photograph.

The men were extremely attractive.

They appeared to be unloading a large item from the back of a car, but the image was fuzzy and both men seemed to be caught off guard looking at the camera.

"You want more tea?" Calder asked, nuzzling my neck.

How in the hell had I gone from lonely carpenter with only memories of this man to cuddling in front of a fire, accepting soft kisses, and wondering if this project was the beginning of something so much bigger and better than either of us had ever dreamed?

"No, I'm good." I reached for the diary, but paused to brush my lips over his. "I'm really glad you're here with me."

"Glad you're here with me, too. Definitely wouldn't be doing all this creepy shit on my own." Calder chuckled. "Sorry, Presley. Brock is the braver of the two."

Opening the diary, again careful to keep my fingers from smearing the pages, I began to read.

August 27, 1918

I found my father dead today.

He had hung himself from the ceiling beam in his mortuary clinic.

Until today, I never dared to write about my experiences with my father for fear he would find my words.

However, due to his passing, I no longer have that fear.

After taking care of the body and reporting his death to the police. Although, does one report a life cut short by suicide to the authorities? Yes, I suppose I must. After doing what must be done, I think I shall fill the lonely hours with writing.

And I shall request someone else deal with Father's body.

His clinic, his obsession with death and the deceased, his frightful collection of ventriloquist dolls, all of them are more than I care to be involved with.

September 19, 1918

It has been nearly a month since finding my father hung.

I had thought to write, but dealing with his death took up too much of my time.

I am in my eighteenth year and did not imagine I would ever be tasked with putting my father to rest.

I do hope he can now rest.

With Mother.

While I never knew her, and I might as well have never known my father, I do hope they are together now in the great beyond or wherever it is spirits go.

There are spirits here.

In this house.

This lonely old house.

I used to hear Father speaking to the spirits.

Now he's gone and the spirits remain. As if they are stuck here.

I do hope to write more in the coming days.

October 1, 1918

I have finally sold the majority of Father's tools and materials.

I sold the old wagon he used to use to transport bodies into town.

With the money from these sales, I purchased a petrol-powered automobile. I do fear I shall miss the wagon, but I still have my bicycle along with the automobile.

I have opted to keep the house.

It is mine free and clear.

There are no truly happy memories here, however, it remains the only home I have ever known.

July 26, 1919

My plans to write have become laughable.

Who will ever read these words?

What is the reason for writing them?

Will someone in the future desire to know of my father's oddities?

Will this person long to know how secluded I was until I turned twelve years?

My only contact with people being on our trips into town to deliver bodies.

For twelve years, my education had been at my father's side as he passed along arithmetic, chemistry, and business skills. Father claimed I got my penmanship and writing talent from Mother.

Upon turning twelve, I realized other children went to school in town.

I begged Father to let me attend school and he relented so long as I delivered bodies to churches and funeral homes for him. Father never enjoyed the delivery trips to town; always more content with his bodies, his dolls, and the spirits.

I feel as if it were a strange sight to see a small boy delivering deceased bodies, however, it was such a freedom for me and I took my job and subsequent schooling very seriously.

School taught me much.

One lesson I learned quickly was just how strange my father was.

He was less than sociable which I knew from how grumpy he would get on delivery days before I took over the job.

However, he truly had very little desire to interact with townsfolk.

And they appeared to feel the same.

Many people avoided him based on his obsession with death and constant discussion of the deceased.

His penchant for the new art of throwing one's voice, and the frightful dolls one used in this artform, was much too disturbing for many. While Father didn't do well with friendly chatter, he could talk at length about ventriloquism. However, he never seemed to master the skill, just had a strange obsession with the artform and the dolls.

For six years, I helped Father as needed, attended school, worked odd jobs in town, and assumed my life would continue as such.

Discovering my deceased father in his mortuary had not been part of my plans, but I would be a liar to say it saddened me.

Perhaps I was fearful of how I would go on.

However, I knew even then, I would not miss the man.

I feel as if there is not much else to say.

Perhaps I will write again when words strike me.

January 13, 1922

My last entry stated I would write if words struck me.

I have been struck.

Clare struck me and words of love abound.

I came across my dearest Clare during the harvest months of 1921.

Clare Smith had run from a less than favorable existence at home and needed a place to stay.

While it was not the most conventional or acceptable situation, I extended a welcome to Clare.

Perhaps because I was lonely.

Perhaps because I was starved for love and touch and friendship.

Clare and I fell into an easy routine as boarder and host, and as friends.

We share chores.

We share meals.

We share the small payments we bring in from doing small jobs in and around town.

Clare has quickly become to mean very much to me.

"P and C," Calder whispered as he took my hand.

"But who is Ren? P hearts Ren?"

"Keep reading."

We scanned a couple random entries, but Presley only wrote about Clare.

"Whoa, there's *Ren*," Calder said, his finger hovering over the page.

September 1, 1922

The unfairness of life sometimes sneaks up on me.

I lost a father I barely knew, yet I never really felt the sting.

I lost a mother I never met. I feel we would have been close, but that may just be my wishful thinking.

None of those two happenings in my life have shaken me as deeply as falling in love with my dearest Ren.

Will future readers be interested in my sad love story?

Will they want to know about the odd mortician widower's lonely son falling in love with a wandering and outcast man?

. . .

My heart caught in my throat as the words spilled from my tongue.

Perhaps I may never shout this love from the rooftops as we are told we are heathens, taboo, sinners of the worst kind.

However, I have known loneliness.

I have known the hollowness of being unloved, unwanted, unnoticed.

The happiness I have found with Clarence Edgar Smith is the absolute most wonderful feeling I've ever experienced.

He is my forever.

My ecstasy.

My love.

My reason for breathing.

Reason for existing.

Reason for carrying on.

My Clare.

My Ren.

My Ren has brought sunshine to my life.

My Ren has given me hope for a future.

Perhaps our future requires a hidden love until one day when we can rejoice in what we have found together.

But that is acceptable.

I will put up with whatever I must in order to keep Ren in my life.

What we share with each other is too good, too special, too overwhelming to think it could ever be wrong or taboo or a sin.

I shall keep our love sheltered and protected in this home from here until eternity.

We are always careful.

Folks in town seem to believe Clarence is a boarder. Down on his luck and grateful for a place to call home with an orphaned man just looking for a bit of money to live on.

Perhaps townsfolk will begin to wonder, begin to question and talk.

Ren and I do not often go to town together.

We do not speak of each other unless directly asked.

We downplay our friendship and focus on the fact Clarence needed a place to live and I needed the fee he pays for boarding.

However, Clarence, my Ren, is so much more to me.

He is a fire in my blood.

Whispered words of love.

Soft caresses of skin.

Hard, rough kisses and coupling.

Gentle lovemaking.

Without him, I would surely be lost.

With him, with my Ren, my life makes sense.

Perhaps we will forever live in secret, but if my heart belongs to Ren, I shall not care for the secrecy.

I will never understand how what Ren and I share could be thought of as wrong.

If only others could feel the love we have for each other.

If only they could understand that we are the same breath, we are the same heart, we are the same being.

If they understood that we mean no harm to anyone else

and we only wish to live our love in peace, maybe we could escape the constant fear.

October 30, 1922

Ren is terrified he's been found.

He went into town to pick up supplies and the grocer mentioned two men had been asking about a Clarence Smith.

Ren feels the description of these two men means his father and uncle have tracked him down.

The grocer, a kind man who hears all but has always treated us fairly, indicated the strangers were saying quite derogatory things to anyone who would listen.

Ren raced home and has been tense ever since.

He is worried his family will come here for him.

They threatened to kill him when he was caught with another man.

Ren only escaped their threats by running.

He has been on the run from them—from his family—for years.

He is tired, he is scared, and he is fighting the urge to run again.

If he runs, if he leaves, I will not survive his absence.

Can I run with him?

Here, in my father's home, we have shelter. We are fed, warm, and surrounded by our love.

If we run, where will we go?

Where will we be allowed to share a home, a bed, a life?

If we stay, what terrors will his family bring upon us?

I would rather die than be without Ren, but I fear the outcome of his family finding him.

He claims his father and uncle are the worst kind of men and have no qualms about maiming and killing that which they do not understand.

Perhaps we should run.

But where?

Where can I take my dear Ren and protect him?

Where can we go and still be afforded our privacy? Still share our love?

My heart aches to watch my dearest so distraught and afraid.

My heart aches at the thought of losing what we have together.

My blood runs cold thinking of him being scared or hurt.

Ren feels he must leave to protect me.

I feel I cannot stand to think of him running, alone.

What can I do to protect him? To protect our love? To save our future?

eight
calder

"OH GOD. Don't stop, keep going."

Brock's distraught eyes met mine. "That's it. The diary ends. There's nothing more."

"Fuck," I growled out, fear and despair filling my chest. "Maybe they ran and forgot the diary." I knew it was unlikely. Deep down, I knew that diary ended because Ren and Presley ended.

But how?

When?

What happened?

Why was Presley here in the house and Ren was not?

"Presley?" Brock whispered to the room. "Can you tell us what happened?"

To the side of the fireplace, the air shimmered and a faint image of a man appeared.

Reaching for Brock's hand, I took hold and squeezed, so grateful for his warm presence. "Presley?"

The spirit nodded with a smile. "It has taken me years and years to learn how to use this ghostly body. In the beginning, I was so lost, so distraught, so alone. I spent many years wallowing in the pits of despair. Learning to open and close windows, blow out candles, move objects, those came with a lot of determination and time to practice."

"Um, would you like to sit?" Brock offered, gesturing toward the couch.

"No, thank you. Speaking is a newer skill and allowing myself to be seen takes a lot of focus."

"Can you tell us what happened and how we can help?" I asked. My gut told me the story wasn't happy, but I still wasn't seeing what part we played in Presley's situation.

"I've never told this story. I shall try to get through." Presley's image flickered as if his power source wavered. Perhaps he feared telling his story.

"You and Ren loved each other very much, yeah?" I asked, hoping to let him know Brock and I were on his side. "Clare? Clarence?"

Presley chuckled with no humor, only a fondness. "Clarence was my one true love and I must get to him. I've been stuck here for a hundred years on Halloween. The time passes slowly, but also in the blink of an eye. I carry on with such guilt and regret and despair, but the spirit world brought you here to save me, to reunite me with my Ren."

He walked from one side of the fireplace to the other. "I started that diary because I was lonely. I did not *miss* my father—he was lost in his own world and had no time for a child—but after finding him dead, I realized just how very alone I was. The words I wrote were to keep me company. I had a thought I would go back and read what I had written and shake my head at how far I had come. But I found I lacked any inspiration for writing. Until Ren."

"Can you tell us what happened?"

Presley continued. "When I first met Clarence, I thought him the most beautiful creature in the world. I had a very limited life experience, but I immediately knew I wanted to spend time with him, call him my friend, and get to know him."

My gut churned as Presley described how I felt about Brock way back then. But I had run from those feelings, lied to myself and everyone around me just to escape the fear of anyone knowing I was gay.

Fuck.

What a coward I'd been.

Presley lived in a time where prison and death were consequences of others knowing about one's sexuality.

I lived during a time where I'd have likely taken some flack, but I didn't face death.

And still, I'd run.

Presley had stayed and fallen in love with his Ren.

"Clarence—I started calling him Clare in my diary as a way to protect his identity. Later, I switched to Ren because it was my own small way of shouting our love from the rooftops even though I could not truly claim our love. He had run from his family after they'd found him with a man. He needed a place to stay. I had an entire house. No one really knew my financial situation, so the story of needing money from a boarder was plausible."

We'd gathered a lot of this from the diary, but I got the feeling Presley needed to ease into telling us what happened to him and Ren.

"Ren and I fell in love very quickly. He had always known he found men attractive. I had never once given it any thought. I knew the expectation was a man would take a wife and fill a home with children, but I was usually looked upon as the odd mortician's son and no girls were giggling in corners hoping I would come calling." Presley smiled ruefully, shaking his head at an unspoken memory. "The moment Ren came to live with me, I realized he was the person I had been waiting on my entire life even though I had never known I was seeking love."

I squeezed Brock's hand again. Way back then, I wasn't looking for love. Wasn't ready for love. Didn't know or accept myself enough to tackle a relationship —at least not in a way that would give the relationship a chance to thrive.

But now?

Just like Presley, I didn't come to Prairie Brook seeking a second chance at love.

I came for a job.

A chance to reinvent myself.

And I found Brock.

Would we get that second chance?

Had we changed too much?

Or had we changed just enough?

I cast a brief smile Brock's way.

All I knew was that connection between us from so long ago was most definitely still there.

And I wanted that second chance.

Wanted to grab it, hold tight, and never let go.

But would I get that chance?

Or had I messed up with Brock when I ran away?

Brock returned the squeeze and smile.

Presley continued.

"It was Halloween of 1922 when a knock sounded at the door. The hour was late and Ren was warm, curled in my arms as we slept. But the knocking persisted and loud voices added to the noise. We got up, dressing quickly and quietly. Ren wrapped his arms around me in a hug that felt as if he were already saying goodbye. My dear Ren whispered his love for me and made me promise we'd be together always. Of course, I readily agreed—he was the love of a lifetime and I'd never leave him."

Presley grew quiet.

"Or so I thought." He was pacing by this point. "I ushered Ren to the kitchen and told him to stay hidden. My plan was to get rid of the intrusion and be back in bed within the hour. I think I knew my plan would easily go askew, but I held tight to hope."

He took a shuddering breath, steeling himself to go on.

"Upon opening the door, I found two men. They

introduced themselves as William and Edgar Smith, Clarence's father and uncle. Said there had been a misunderstanding between the family, their dear Clarence had run off, and they simply wanted to speak to him and clear the air.

"For one brief moment, I wanted to believe their lies, but something in my gut told me Clarence was in danger. I informed the men I did not know of a Clarence Smith."

Presley's image flickered and I worried we'd lose him before he could finish the story.

"His father got very angry. Told me he knew exactly what had been going on between his son and me. Said he would leave me be as long as I turned over Clarence."

Presley shook his head.

"Ren had never been very good at sticking with a plan or being told what to do. He emerged from the kitchen claiming his love for me and how he'd rather die than live without me."

He breathed deeply, barely suppressing a sob.

"And I betrayed him. Fear over losing him, fear for myself—truly, I had never been so afraid—I denied my dear Ren. I told his father and uncle we were simply friends helping each other out in a difficult situation. I told them of losing my mother and father, told them of trying to keep the house going on my own, and how grateful I was for a friend like Clarence to help with the upkeep and finances.

"I will never forget the look of betrayal on my dear

Ren's face. All I wanted to do was make the men leave and spend the rest of my life making it up to him. But Ren, my dear, distraught, betrayed Ren, he faced his father and uncle. Told them he would *never* betray who he was, he would *never* be associated with the evil within them."

Presley's form wavered, flickering heavily.

"They shot him in the back as he ran from the house," Presley whispered hoarsely. "He made it as far as our tree before falling in a heap. I remember very little after that, but I do recall chasing after him, screaming when he was shot, and collapsing next to Ren's lifeless body as sobs wracked my soul. I had done the one thing I had always said I would never do. I had betrayed him. I had denied our love. The one person in the entire world who understood me, loved me, and wanted a future with me—no matter how secret and hidden we had to be—I had claimed him as only a friend, denied what we meant to each other, and betrayed him in his greatest time of need. He died thinking I did not love him. He died with only the knowledge of my betrayal.

"Ren's uncle stood over us, evil lurking in his eyes as he pointed his gun at me. *My nephew was a damn sinner and monstrosity and you ain't no better. You two deserve to rot in hell for your sins.*

"He shot me then. I remember the searing pain of the bullet ripping through my flesh, but I recall the pain of betraying Ren being the worst I had ever felt. I believe I choked to death on my own blood, but worse than suffocating a slow death, I lost Ren that night. Lost him to death and betrayal. Lost my true love when I was too much of a coward to claim him as mine. Lost him to hatred and bigotry. And now I walk alone. You two are the closest I have come to having hope in ninety-nine years; you will be the key to sending me beyond the veil."

"What can we do?" I asked.

But Presley's already faint image flickered and disappeared.

"Please forgive me. I am so very tired. I shall return when I have regained my strength. Please do not abandoned me. You are my only hope. Halloween."

"Fuck," Brock mumbled. "God, I knew that was going to end sadly, but I wasn't really ready for it. They were murdered. Cold-blooded murder. All because of who they loved."

I pressed a kiss to Brock's head and stood from our place on the floor, heading to the kitchen with a jumble of thoughts in my head, our empty tea mugs in hand, and a heavy heart.

Returning to our bedroom—fuck, *our* bedroom…I'd gone and gotten myself in deep—I heard water running in the bathroom. Rifling through the stack of photographs, I found the one of Presley and Ren.

It wasn't a posed picture.

Not planned.

They didn't have the luxury of asking a photographer to take their picture as any opposite-sex couple might have done. In fact, the two men's look of surprise mingled with fear in the image.

Fearful of rumors about their relationship?

Fearful of Ren's family finding him?

Again, I recalled my past fears.

My fear had been real and true, but Presley's story had driven home the fact that I hadn't known the same struggles.

Yes, we unfortunately still lived in a time where a person's very identity could be shamed and harmed.

And those in the LGBTQ+ community truly had every right to still be fearful—lives were destroyed daily because of the hatred that still filled the world.

I couldn't speak for others because their lived experiences weren't mine, but I knew without a doubt that my fears of the past weren't based on true dangers. I was scared of what people would think of me. Not prison or torture or death; those things weren't realities *I* faced.

Tossing the photograph on the mantle, I leaned on my elbows, face in hands, bracing myself against the old wood.

I wasn't sure how Presley thought Brock and I could help him, but I was willing to do whatever he needed if it meant saving him from this lonely existence and reuniting him with his Ren.

And I was determined to rectify the decisions of my past.

I didn't know the how or why behind what brought Brock and I together in this time and place, but I knew with one hundred percent certainty that we were being given a second chance.

I was being given a second chance.

To make things right.

To be true to myself.

To love the one man I'd never been able to shake loose from my mind, no matter how hard I tried.

"Hey, you okay?" Brock asked, his closeness a comforting warmth.

Reaching for him, I backed him to the wall, one hand wrapped around the back of his neck, the other cupping his face.

"Calder?" Brock asked, longing and desire flaming to life in his eyes, but a questioning look all the same.

"Need you," was all I got out before slamming my lips to his and devouring his mouth.

Brock groaned, opening for me, accepting my plunging tongue, and returning the kiss with as much ferocity as it was given.

I knew I should stop and tell him what I was feeling, but the need was too strong. Scratch the itch first, talk about how Presley's story was fuckin' with my head later.

"What do you want?" I asked, my lips whispering over his as we rocked our engorged cocks together.

"Anything," Brock answered. "Just want you, that hasn't changed."

Maybe it was because of the guilt and regret of using him in the past or running away from my feelings, but I needed to give myself to Brock.

Longed to give myself to him.

Yeah, in a fucked up, round-about way it was a chance to right a wrong.

Mostly, it was me living out a fantasy.

But I needed him inside me like I needed my next breath.

"Fuck me," I growled before biting his lip and reigniting the kiss. "Wanna feel you inside me." Cupping his rock-hard cock, I groaned and moved us toward the bed.

Brock reached for the drawer and tossed lube on the bed. Holding up a foil packet, he cocked a brow. "Probably not the best time to be having this conversation, but I swear you've got my head scrambled. Do we need this?"

For a moment, my brain short-circuited. Brock Shelton asking if I was okay with him fucking me bare? It was like every single one of my fantasies coming true.

I shook my head. "I'm good. Negative tests all around and not been with anyone since my last one. You?"

"Same. I'm on board either way, just wanted to put it out there."

"We're good." My ass clenched in anticipation when Brock tossed the condom back in the drawer and slammed it shut.

"Just so you know, going without isn't something I normally do." Brock eyed me as he pushed down his pants and underwear, his steely shaft smacking against his belly.

"Same. And by *not normally*, I mean never." For some reason, admitting that felt like something big. Hell, having sex with someone without protection was huge. But I trusted Brock.

This was more than just sex.

I wasn't ready to name it.

Had no real ideas on where it might be going—or at least not ideas I was willing to examine right then.

And maybe it was the fact we had a past together—despite the fact the past was kinda shitty.

But Brock and me falling into bed together wasn't just a hookup or way to pass the time.

It was real.

And in reality, it both scared the shit out of me and sent my heart soaring.

But those were things we could deal with later.

"Yeah, me too," he answered, his voice gruff.

Pushing him to the bed, I knelt between his legs and took his cock between my lips. The idea of being on my knees as he fucked my face was something I'd gotten off to more times than I could count. Back then, I wanted nothing more than to suck him off, but fear and stereotypes kept me from doing it.

Now though, I had no problem with it.

Except the fact I was a greedy bastard and needed him sliding into my ass.

Standing, I stripped off my clothes, tossing them aside before I straddled him. Wrapping my arms around him, groaning at the warm heat of his strong arms around my waist, I welcomed his soul-searing kiss.

When he shifted our bodies and pushed my back to the mattress, I grunted and fisted my cock.

For a brief moment, it seemed as if Brock wanted to talk.

Honestly, we likely *should* have discussed some things, but the fire in my blood for this man was at a boiling point.

Talking could wait.

"Fuck me," I demanded.

"Bossy," Brock teased.

"Fuck me, *please*," I amended.

He chuckled and positioned himself on his stomach. Lifting my ass and spreading my cheeks, Brock swiped his tongue over my hole. "This okay?"

"God, yeah." If not for the tight grip on my cock, I probably would have shot my load right then and there. But I fisted myself and groaned, giving in to the sensation of his warm, wet tongue rimming and fucking my ass.

"Fuck," I bit out several moments later, "need you in me."

Brock grabbed the lube and smeared his fingers along with my sensitive hole. He slipped one finger into my ass, followed quickly by two.

I braced my feet on the bed and rocked my ass, fucking myself on his fingers. Bottoming wasn't my go-to. I'd had sex with a handful of men and the majority of them expected—usually, demanded—I be the one fucking them. But letting Brock fuck me had been on the top of my spank bank fantasy list since I was old enough to know anything about sex.

So, the sting of his fingers opening me up, the fullness, the tight grip of my muscle around his thick digits was a dream come true.

But I wanted more.

"Please," I murmured.

"Roll over," Brock commanded.

With crazy-hot—equal emphasis on *crazy* and *hot*—images of a future filled with Brock bossing me around in bed, I rolled to my stomach and lifted my hips.

Brock left the bed just long enough to grab a towel and spread it under me. "Gotta think of the laundry," he said with a quick kiss before lubing his cock and kneeling between my spread thighs.

The silky soft comforter teased my tight nipples and I rocked my ass backwards. With my legs spread and ass lifted, only the tip of my cock brushed against the towel, but the friction drove me mad.

Brock pressed the blunt head of his cock against my hole and I bit my lip to keep from begging him to just wreck me. Pushing back against his intrusion, I groaned as the tight ring of muscle relaxed just enough to allow his thick shaft to slide in. The burning sting took my breath away, but Brock held still long enough for my body to adjust to his perfect cock. "Fuck, that's good," I mumbled into the comforter.

"Relax your hips," Brock said, his big rough hands guiding me to lie prone on the mattress as he shifted and spread his entire body over mine, his hot, thick cock still buried in my throbbing hole. "This okay?" he murmured against my ear, his warm chest pressing against my back as he swirled his hips, driving his dick deeper into my body.

"Fuck, yeah," I bit out, followed by a moan when he pulled almost all the way out before driving back into me in long, slow thrusts. I spread my legs just enough to allow his to slot between and he braced himself on his elbows before pumping his hips, each stroke of his cock filling me with heated desire just waiting to explode.

The press of his hips against my backside pushed my cock into the towel and I found myself grunting and rutting like a damn teen just learning the joys of friction. With my senses on overload—the scent of sex and Brock all around me, the warm press of his arms caging me to the mattress, the porn-worthy grunts and groans dancing with the pops and hisses of the fire—I gave myself to the sensations.

Never before had sex been this good.

And I knew in my heart it wasn't just the sex.

It was the man.

My ass clenched around his fat cock, my balls begging to unload, sweat dripping from my brow... none of those things were surprising in the least.

It was sex after all.

But my heart?

The warm swirl of emotions making their presence known as they fluttered through my chest?

Those were different.

Those were the game changer.

"Fuck, I'm close," Brock growled in my ear. "Wanna feel you come on my cock and then shoot my load in this pretty ass."

His gruff words and harsh breathing, coupled with his thrusting hips and the lightning bolts flashing through me each time his cock brushed my prostate, had me reaching for my shaft. With a tight grip and only three strokes, I moaned as my orgasm washed over me, spurting hot cum over my fist and onto the waiting towel.

The release had my ass clenching tightly around Brock's shaft and he slammed into me once more, stilling with a grunt as his cock throbbed in my hole. Each pulse of his dick shooting his cum deep in my ass sent a shiver through me as I continued to ride out my orgasm.

Brock finally collapsed onto me, his body a welcome weight. He pressed a kiss along my jaw, but when I turned my head slightly, he claimed my mouth in a kiss hot enough to have my cock valiantly attempting a resurgence. Licking into his sweet mouth, I savored the taste of him on my tongue, the soft touch of his fingers buried in my hair.

We slowly ended the kiss, breathing heavily, sated and heavy-lidded.

"Holy fuck," I panted into the mattress. "That was at least fifty-percent of my teenage fantasies come true."

Brock chuckled. "Only half?"

"I mean, the other half consisted of me drilling that sweet ass of yours."

We were quiet for a moment.

"So, just teenage fantasies?" Brock asked, his body pressed against my side, breath tickling over my ear.

A residual shudder rippled through me as his cum leaked from my ass. "Yeah, okay, maybe some more recent fantasies as well," I mumbled.

"We wanna talk about any of this?"

"Is there anything to talk about?" I huffed. "I mean, there's plenty to talk about, I'm just not sure my head has wrapped around any of it enough to make much sense."

"So, just fuck buddies until Halloween and then we go our separate ways?" Brock suggested, a bit of bite to his words.

I pulled him close for a kiss, dipping my tongue between his lips, absorbing his gruff moan. "You scrambled my brain good, but I think we both know this feels like more than that."

Brock sighed into the kiss.

"Let's clean up, sleep, and kick ass on some projects tomorrow. Hopefully Presley comes back and we can get some answers about helping him."

"And whatever this is?" Brock asked.

"I think it's safe to say it's some kind of thing—

sorry, I don't really have words for it right now. Maybe we just let it simmer, enjoy it, see where it goes?"

"Yeah, okay. That's doable." Brock pressed a kiss to my lips and rolled from the bed. After a few moments, he returned with a wet cloth for me.

Once cleaned up, we settled into bed.

I loved the press of our warm naked limbs tucked comfortably under the blanket as the low fire filled the room with a soft light and cozy warmth.

"He'll come back, right?" Brock asked.

"I hope so. He said he would. Seemed like showing himself and telling us his story took a lot out of him. Probably just needs some time to regroup, build up strength. I'm sure reliving his story was painful as well as exhausting."

"He seems so sure we can help. I think I'm scared to hear what he thinks we can do; scared to find out we can't really help." Brock held my hand, pressing our joined fingers against his chest.

Brushing a kiss over his hair I sighed. "Yeah, I get that. I guess we just have to wait. At least we know he's got a date in mind and it's not far away. And we've got work to keep us busy until then."

"Their chance was ripped away from them," Brock mumbled, his words growing sleepy. "I can't even imagine the stress and fear of their love back then, but what they had was so real. It *had* to be. No one would go through what they went through if what they felt for each other wasn't overwhelmingly real and soul-deep."

My heart lodged in my throat. "They were brave. They fought for their love." A shudder traveled through me. "Presley's despair and regret is like a punch to the gut. I *get* those feelings because I lived them."

Brock rolled in my arms, propping his head on his bent arm. "What?"

"When I denied my attraction toward guys," I paused, pressing my forehead to his and whispering a kiss over his mouth, "when I ran away from what I felt for *you*, I did the same as Presley. Maybe I didn't do it to save you like he tried to save Ren. Hell, maybe you didn't even know I left because of my feelings toward you. But I denied the real me and I ran. That hurt me and any chance we might have had back then." Nuzzling my nose against Brock's, I breathed in the scent of the man I was sure I'd gone and fallen for all over again. "We had a better outcome...and that's likely *only* because of the time we live in...but I get Presley's regret and how the despair haunts him. I can't imagine the pain of losing the man he loved...knowing that Ren died thinking Presley had denied what they had together."

Tucking Brock against my chest, I kissed the top of his head. "You were so like Ren. You would have shouted it from the rooftops if you'd been in love with someone. Can you imagine just how badly it would have hurt to have loved someone enough to want the whole world to know, but in your time of greatest need—when you were seriously scared for your life—that one person shrugged off the greatest love you've ever known?" Nearly choking on the words, trying to find my way through the emotions, I held Brock tighter.

"I hear what you're saying, I do. But I'd like to think Ren understood Presley was just trying to protect him. Their situation wasn't like our high school years. If you and I had taken things further—past the sneaking around a few times—and I'd wanted everyone to know about us and you'd denied what we had, it would have hurt for sure. Back then, I wasn't in a position to understand your need to hide. Which is probably why it's for the best you left for a while. Gave us both a chance to grow into the men we were meant to be, experience life and love, get to know ourselves." Brock's voice held the edge of sleep and I knew it wouldn't be long before he slipped into slumber. "I absolutely can't imagine the fear and desperation Presley and Ren experienced back then. Scared for their lives, scared to lose what they'd spent so long protecting. But I really do understand why Presley said what he said. The only thing he wanted to do was get the men to leave and keep Ren by his side. They were so young. They were overpowered, the laws were against them, and they were dealing with true evil." He yawned. "If anything, I'm thinking Ren has probably spent all of the years since his death regretting that Presley is in such despair. I don't think Ren blames Presley at all. I think Ren's biggest regret is that they aren't together."

For a moment, I processed Brock's words, hope

flaring to life in my chest, my heart soaring with emotion.

"At least, that's how I'd feel if I was in their situation." Brock snuggled deeper in my arms. "It's how I feel about us, too. I wouldn't have wanted you to be sad. I mean, maybe I hoped you missed me, but the older I got, the more I realized I didn't really blame you for leaving. You had to do what was best for *you*. We already know those kids we were back then wouldn't have known how to deal with a real relationship. Second chances are special and I think we should take advantage of the one we've been given."

Brock fell silent for a moment and I thought he'd drifted off to sleep.

"Don't want my biggest regret years from now to be that we wasted it and we aren't together. We're not those kids anymore. We can learn from the past," he whispered.

Learn from the past.

Our past?

Presley's and Ren's past?

Both?

Brock was right. We weren't those kids anymore

I was a grown man who knew myself inside and out.

And I knew without a doubt I wanted Brock Shelton in my life from here on out.

Now, we just needed to finish the house and figure out a way to send Presley beyond the veil to spend the rest of eternity with his Ren.

nine
brock

"What if he doesn't come back? How can we help him if he's not here? We don't even know what he thinks we can do to help him," I grumbled to Calder the day before Halloween.

We'd spent the last couple weeks busting ass to finish the house restoration and we both agreed it looked amazing. Between the decent chunk of cash we'd both earned for taking the job, the bonus for staying on site, and the extra cash incentive for finishing by Halloween, Calder and I were beyond satisfied with the way the project had worked out.

But the house seemed empty without Presley and we'd been worried about him. He hadn't returned since the night he told us about how he and Ren died.

Calder and I were both worried, but it wasn't like we could just pick up the phone and ask him if he was okay.

Our two months at the Prairie Brook house had

turned into one of the most memorable times of my life. We had our routine of grocery shopping, doing a few loads at the laundromat, enjoying quick lunches together, and fixing dinner and sipping beer or cider in the evenings.

Ever since the night Calder asked me to fuck him, we'd been burning up the sheets pretty much sun-down to sun-up. Hard, fast, and dirty was our usual go-to, but we slowed things down from time-to-time also. Honestly, there were times where we just held each other, rutting our cocks together, and giving ourselves over to the pleasure.

Blow jobs, hand jobs, frotting, rimming, and anal were all a part of our arsenal and I was pretty sure I'd never tire of sex with Calder.

I was also sure I'd gone and fallen in love with him.

Night after night as we came together, wrapped in each other's arms, I longed to tell him how I felt, but I wasn't sure we were ready for that declaration.

Then I'd think of Presley and Ren and how they likely would have given anything to have more time to experience their love, and I'd realize I was just being a coward. If I told Calder I loved him and it pushed him away, I'd have to accept that what we'd shared over the last two months had been great but we weren't on the same page.

If I kept my words to myself, I could enjoy our time together for a little longer.

"He said Halloween," Calder said. "That's tomorrow. He'll be here soon. Finish those Brussels sprouts so we can clean up. I've got plans for our last night together."

My face must have shown disappointment because Calder leaned in to kiss me. "Our last night together *here*. I'd guess we'll see Presley tonight and Crimson Chaos tomorrow."

Doing my best to ignore the fact we had no solid plan for what was happening once we walked away from the project, I crinkled my brow. "Does it seem weird that we've heard *nothing* from Crimson since the very beginning? I mean, he provided the money and Bernard assures us the bonus amounts are safely in his possession. Just seems odd the man wanted such a huge project but hasn't checked in at all."

Calder shrugged. "You met the guy same as me. Anything about him *not* seem odd?"

Chuckling, I finished the sprouts—loving the fact that Calder and I both enjoyed veggies—and helped him clear the table. A quick zing of longing traveled through me as I thought about our future filled with sharing the chores of cooking, cleaning up, and running a business together.

Would we have that?

Did Calder even want a future like that with me?

Or was he only interested in the business portion?

Hell, *was* he even interested in the business offer?

Was I being an idiot to think about bringing him on?

I needed to lay it all out for him and find out what

Calder was thinking. If he wasn't on-board, I needed to prepare my heart.

If he *was* on-board, I needed to prepare myself for...

What?

A business partner?

A lover?

A boyfriend?

All of the above?

Strong arms wrapped around me and a soft kiss tickled my neck. "Why don't you go take your time in the bathroom. I'll finish up here."

Bernard had delivered a much larger, very much appreciated water heater recently, and the ability to take longer *hot* showers was amazing.

A shiver of anticipation jolted through me. I loved topping Calder. I basically loved anything and everything he and I ever did together. But spreading myself for him, opening my body to him, allowing his cock inside while he buried me in pleasure, those things were top of my list of favorite activities to share with Calder.

As I stepped into the shower, warm water washing away the day's work, I recalled the night Calder topped me for the first time. I'd been dreaming of giving myself to him since I was a horny teenager and reality far surpassed my dreams.

It was likely a good thing we were a lot older and more experienced these days because I had a feeling our sexual exploits back then would have paled in comparison to how amazing things were between us now.

Clenching my ass as I remembered Calder working me open, tongue fucking me, and finally—*finally*—pressing his thick, hard shaft into me, I fisted my cock and stroked a few times.

As pumped up as the recollections had me, there was no way I was rubbing one out in the shower by myself when I had Calder on the other side of the bathroom door preparing to do all manner of deliciously dirty things to my ass.

Taking time to clean everything thoroughly, I turned off the water—grateful there was still plenty for Calder—and dried off. I brushed my teeth, wrapped the towel around my waist, and walked out to the bedroom.

Calder met me, grabbing the towel and ripping it from my waist. His teeth nipped at my lips, his tongue soothing away the sting. "Want you naked and ready when I get out of the shower."

My quickly-thickening cock pressed against his jean-clad thigh. "You better make it the fastest shower on record."

Calder's kiss warmed me in the slightly chilled room. He'd added wood to the fire, but it had yet to thoroughly warm the space. "Yes, sir. Washing all the important parts and then your ass is mine."

I groaned into his mouth, savoring the contrast between his dust-covered, clothed body and my damp, naked skin. My body trembled with the sensation.

He chuckled and nudged me toward the bed. "Get under the blankets and warm up."

As the shower came to life, I crawled under the blankets and shivered, grateful the fire was burning hotter.

Calder emerged from the bathroom moments later running a towel through his hair, his thick, heavy cock hanging enticingly between his legs.

My mouth watered as he sauntered to the fireplace and added another log. Shifting the blankets to reveal my naked body, our eyes met and held as he moved closer to the bed, spreading his towel on the mattress.

"Like what you see?" he asked gruffly, stroking himself as his eyes devoured me. He stood at the head of the bed, his hard cock just begging to be sucked.

Reaching for him, I gripped his hip and pulled him flush to the mattress. The scent of soap and Calder filled my senses as my lips stretched around his thick shaft, my tongue swirling around his cockhead, savoring the salty tang of his pre-cum.

Calder's groan filled the air as his hand fisted in my hair, sliding his cock deep into my throat, his eyes filled with heat in the dim glow of the firelight. "Fuck, Brock. You suck me so good. Love those pretty lips around my dick."

I hummed around his shaft and thrust into his fist when he reached to stroke me. Popping off his cock, I yanked Calder to the bed. Our mouths met in a wet, sloppy kiss as his body covered mine, his hips slotting perfectly between my open thighs.

"Gonna suck you while you work yourself open," Calder murmured at my ear before biting the lobe. "Then I'm gonna fill you with my cum and make that pretty ass clench around my cock."

I groaned into his mouth, his dirty words setting me on fire.

Calder shifted, grabbed the lube, and thrust it against my chest.

Fisting my cock, he demanded, "Come on, get that ass ready for my cock. Love watching you finger yourself."

Slicking my fingers, I blindly tossed the lube bottle to the side and shifted my position to smear the viscous liquid over my hole. With one leg bent and my cock in Calder's grip, I breached my opening with a groan.

"Fuck, yeah. Do two," Calder murmured, stroking my shaft, his eyes glued to my ass where I worked a second finger into my tight muscle. "You want my cock in there?"

I grunted in answer and stretched myself, knowing I needed the prep before I could comfortably take Calder's thick dick.

Calder fondled my balls before moving to press kisses up my torso, landing on my mouth with a deep, promising kiss. "Get on your hands and knees." His low, demanding words sent fire through my blood.

With my cock leaking, I moved to the position he requested, knowing my slick, open hole was on display for him to see as I spread my legs and pressed my chest to the mattress.

"Fucking hell, I love your ass," Calder grumbled as he moved between my legs, slapping his hard length against my waiting hole. "Anyone ever tell you you've got these two perfect dimples right here?" He stroked his thumbs over the skin just above my ass. "It's like they were made just for me. My thumbs fit perfectly while I grip your hips and fuck your pretty ass."

Shivering, loving the words he spoke, picturing his thumbs swirling over the dimples, his fingers gripping hard enough to mark me, I pressed my ass toward him. "Fuck, Calder, get in me already."

He chuckled while lubing himself. "Patience. I'll make it worth it."

"You always do," I mumbled into the mattress. Despite our short and somewhat messy past, Calder—the man he was now—liked to take care of me. Not that I *needed* taking care of, but it was a feeling that made my insides all warm and gooey.

The blunt press of his cockhead had me groaning before the brief burning sting took my breath away. Calder's thumbs ran circles over the small of my back, one hand stroking up and down my spine. "You good?"

In answer, I rocked back on his cock. "So good. Fill me up."

He began a hard and fast thrusting rhythm and all too soon my balls were drawn tight. Calder bent over me, wrapped an arm around my chest, and shifted us to a kneeling position, never once stopping the sweet, satisfying slide of his cock deep in my ass.

"Fuck, *fuck*," he panted, nipping my neck, slamming his hips into me. "I'm gonna come."

Grunting, I reached down to stroke myself. "Give it to me. Wanna feel your cum in me."

My orgasm ripped through me, my load spilling over my fist as my ass clenched around Calder's cock. With a growl in my ear, he tensed, his dick throbbing inside as warmth filled me.

We collapsed to the mattress and Calder yanked the towel from the bed and wiped us up as best he could before collecting me in his arms and pressing a kiss to my mouth. "Gotta sleep. Showers after a much slower round two," he murmured against my lips.

As we drifted off to sleep, I swore I heard footsteps from somewhere in the house.

Maybe Presley was back.

As much of a pain as he'd been in the beginning, I felt a connection to him now that we'd heard his story. I wanted nothing more than to help him.

Even if I had no clue how we'd do it.

I awoke some time later to a wicked heat engulfing my cock. The half moon shone brightly through the window and the tiny bedside alarm clock showed it was after midnight.

"Fuck, never get tired of your mouth on me," I mumbled, my wrecked ass clenching at the thought of round two.

Calder popped off my cock and spread his body

over mine, our warm chests pressing together. He tasted of me and I groaned into his kiss. "Are you too sore? Or can you take me again?" he whispered against my mouth. "I wanna slide into your ass and know it's my cum making you slick."

"Fuck," I moaned. "I'm good, just go slow." The thought of my ass filled with his earlier load and his thick shaft sliding into me again was enough to have my balls already tingling.

Calder shifted back on his knees and took his solid length in hand, running a thumb over his leaking slit. Guiding his cockhead to my hole, he pressed his shaft slowly into my body. "Oh fuck," he moaned. "Love feeling you slick with my load." He sank all the way in, his balls pressing against me. "You good?"

I reached up, my heart stuttering as Calder took my hand, never stopping the slow, gentle thrusts of his hips. Pulling him toward me, I whimpered slightly, spreading my legs to take him deeper as his chest pressed into mine. Gripping the back of his neck, I kissed him. Long, slow, and deep. My tongue thrust between his lips in the same rhythm as his cock in my ass.

I'd never made love before.

I'd fucked.

I'd had amazing sex.

But this was different.

Emotions and thoughts melded together, swirling in my head and heart, yearning to burst out and be known.

Fear.

Lust.

Promise.

Forever.

Love.

Love.

Love.

"Calder, I…" I murmured against his lips.

Rocking into me, oh-so-slow and gentle, Calder braced on his elbows, his hands holding my face as he pressed our foreheads together. "I love you," he whispered reverently. "God, I love you." His thumbs brushed over my cheeks, his lips dotted soft kisses on my eyelids, my nose, my chin.

A crazy little surprised, happy chuckle escaped me. "I love you, too."

Calder—never taking his eyes from mine—continued his slow thrusting, his abdomen trapping my cock between our bodies, rubbing my shaft to the point of detonation. He shifted his arms, anchoring them under my shoulders, and buried his face in my neck.

We came together in a litany of soft words, promising kisses, and warm, comforting touches.

This time, when Calder grabbed a towel, we did a somewhat better job of cleaning up. It was our last day in the house, the sheets would have to be stripped anyway.

We both needed a shower, but our bodies were too drained to do much other than cuddle together and enjoy the last bit of sleep before sunrise.

"I meant it, you know," Calder whispered against my temple. "I think I've loved you forever. I'm sorry it took so long for me to figure it out." He tipped my chin up and kissed me. "I love you."

"Pretty sure I'll never get tired of hearing that. And I meant it, too." I let our lips linger together. "No apologies. You and I both know what we have now isn't what we would have had then. We needed these years to figure shit out and get ourselves to this point before we could love like this." I sighed, tucking my head into his neck. "Love you," I whispered.

As if the plates of the planet shifted right under us, the entire house shook and an indescribable sound shuddered around us.

"What the fuck was that?" Calder asked.

Scrambling out of bed, yanking on whatever jeans and shirts we grabbed from the floor, Calder and I took off through the house.

"This house is solid and strong, nothing about what just happened makes sense. Earthquake?" I asked. They weren't unheard of in our area, but they were considered rare. And the...*whatever* had just happened...didn't feel *or* sound like any earthquake I'd been through.

"Presley? You here?" Calder called out.

As we moved to the kitchen, I glanced out the back window and froze.

"Calder," I whispered. "Calder, look."

His eyes swung to where mine were focused.

Slowly, not wanting to possibly disturb what I

thought we were seeing, I took his hand and we made our way to the backyard.

There, just beyond the tree where Presley and Ren had carved their initials—where they'd died just for loving each other all those years ago—were two men. Holding hands in the moonlight, dressed in old-fashioned clothes, they smiled, one of them raising his hand in a wave.

We reached the tree and I couldn't help the shiver of happiness. The satisfied sigh from Calder indicated he felt the same. He'd found his way over the veil.

"Presley?" I asked.

"Thank you," Presley said. His voice was soft but strong and he spoke with a relieved confidence we hadn't seen in the brief time we'd known him. "Because of you, I'm reunited with my Ren." He held up their joined hands.

Ren nodded. "Pleased to make your acquaintance."

"I'm so happy for you both," I said. "But I don't understand how we made any of this happen."

Presley cocked his head to the side and studied us. "Ren died thinking I had denied him, turned my back on our love."

"Perhaps for a brief moment," Ren interrupted. "But I knew you were attempting to protect me, to protect *us*. I never held that against you. You were forgiven long before you took your last breath. Your stubborn guilt kept you here for a century."

"Possibly my stubborn guilt. Possibly death's curse. Possibly desperate desire to see love win. Most likely, a strange mixture of the three," Presley explained as if sharing a riddle.

"I'm not following," Calder said.

"I died vowing to atone for denying our love. Upon my death, after much struggle and anguish, I realized I was stuck. Over the years, I convinced myself I could only cross over with three things."

Ren and Presley flickered and I feared we'd lose them before the full story came out.

"Presley and I have been able to converse through the veil over the years. My immediate forgiveness— once we figured out we could speak from time-to-time…especially at Halloween when I'm able to travel freely through the veil—was the first thing Presley needed," Ren explained. "I've spent years upon years trying to convince him to just cross over with me." He sighed and brought their joined hands to his mouth for a kiss. "Whether it was truly death's curse or just his stubborn guilt—"

"Or love looking for just the right place to land," Presley interrupted.

Ren smiled and shook his head. "Who knew my Presley was such a romantic?"

"So, you've had Ren's forgiveness all this time. What else did you need?" Calder asked.

"When the spirits brought you both here, I knew it was time. I'd be reunited with my love and I could spend eternity with him beyond the veil. If we weren't allowed to love and spend our living days growing old and in love, eternity as spirits didn't sound half bad."

Presley glanced at the house. "The other two things I needed were to see love get a second chance—to see love be claimed and not denied—and to see my home filled with that love."

I swallowed thickly as Presley's words sank in.

"Wait, are you saying you were able to cross over because Brock and I fell in love?" Calder asked.

Presley smiled, looking at our joined hands. "I'm not sure it *had* to be the two of you. I knew the moment the spirits brought you here, though. You were my one true hope. From the first day, I watched and listened…"

"And made a nuisance of yourself," I added.

Our matchmaking ghost just smiled and shrugged. "Perhaps. But I heard your story, I knew Calder had denied his feelings—denied *himself*—in the past. I felt the spark between you from the very beginning. I knew, I just *knew*, if you could put aside the past and be true to each other, that tiny seed of love from way back then would take root and grow into something real. I think I've been rooting for you two to find love as much for *you* as for Ren and me." He gazed back at the old house. "That house held no good memories for me until Ren came into my life. I don't want it to sit empty and alone. I believe my mother hoped to fill the home with love and happiness and I want nothing more than for you to do that now."

My heart fell. "Pres, I'm sorry. You know we were just here to restore the place, right?"

He cocked his head. "Were you?"

Ren smiled impishly beside him.

"We'll let you figure that part out," Presley said. "We must go. We have one hundred years of love to make up for and I don't plan to waste a single moment." He stared directly at Calder and me. "Thank you. Thank you for allowing your love a second chance. Thank you for allowing *us* a second chance. Thank you for bringing love into my home. And thank you for being exactly what I needed to cross the veil and find my Ren. I will *never* forget you and I wish you a lifetime of love and happiness, here and beyond."

And with that, Presley and Ren faded from sight.

"Did that just happen?" I whispered.

"I think so. We're not dreaming, right?"

I reached over and pinched his arm.

"Oww!" Calder grumbled.

"Nope, not dreaming." I shivered.

"Let's get inside. It's chilly. We need showers and sleep."

In a daze, as if trying to process everything we'd just heard, Calder and I went through the motions of brushing our teeth and showering.

Naked, clean, and warm, we climbed into bed and wrapped ourselves together.

"What do you think he meant about leaving it to us to figure out? When I reminded him we were just here for the restoration?" I asked.

"No idea. Something about Crimson Chaos?"

"That guy was weird, but he was real, right? We saw

him right here. He paid us real money. No way he was a ghost. Right?" My head was spinning.

"I know nothing about ghosts and spirits. He seemed very real. But we haven't heard a single word from him since taking this job. He's not been here to check on things. Even Bernard hinted he's lost contact with him. Crimson wanted the house done today. I assume he'll show up and kick us out pretty soon." Calder kissed the top of my head.

"If he does?"

"We'll figure it out. We've got business plans to discuss, living arrangements to figure out, and a promising future ahead of us." Calder's voice held a soft anticipation that made my heart soar.

"And if he doesn't?"

He shrugged. "We let Bernard figure that shit out." Calder tipped my chin up for a sleepy kiss. "All I know is we somehow ended up together on this project and it brought us a second chance at what I stupidly walked away from back then. I don't plan on wasting any more time. I love you. Then and now, same and different. I'm not sure there's any love story better than ours."

I sighed contentedly in his arms. "We got our own second chance at love. We helped Presley and Ren reunite. We fixed up this gorgeous home. We're going to spend the rest of our lives as partners in business and in love, loving what we do."

"And doing what—or *who*—we love," Calder teased. "Best love story ever. And this is only chapter one."

"Wasn't way back then chapter one?"

"Nah, that was the prologue. No one reads the prologue."

I gasped and smacked a hand to his chest. "What? No. You *have* to read the prologue. If it's there, you have to read it. It sets the stage and gives you important information."

Calder chuckled. "Okay, fine. Prologue and chapter one." He kissed me, his tongue sweeping in to mate with mine, our morning stubble scratching on our chins. "As long as you let me love you and write chapter after chapter with you from here until the end of time, I'll vow to start reading prologues."

"Deal," I murmured against his lips. "I think second chance romances are going to be my newest guilty pleasure."

Calder hummed and cuddled me down into the mattress, under the warm blankets. "We've got our own second chance romance to live out right here."

"And there's no one else in the world I'd rather write this story with than you." I pressed a last kiss to his lips and curled into him.

We'd sleep.

We'd get in touch with Bernard.

We'd figure shit out.

We'd look toward the future.

And we'd do it all together.

epilogue

Calder

"I think that's probably the last of them," I said, stealing a Twix from the bowl of candy on our front porch. "Tomorrow's a school day, most of the parents likely want the kids home and at least attempting to head to bed."

Brock stood from the porch swing and took my hand. "You're probably right." He blew out the spooky lanterns and jack-o-lanterns, turned off the glowing witch face and wiggling ghost, and led me down the steps. "Let's see if we have visitors."

We walked to the backyard.

Our backyard.

Crimson Chaos never returned. Bernard did some digging two years ago and came to the conclusion the man never existed. Where did the money come from? Who was the man we all saw ask the Ouija board questions? What the heck had happened with that entire situation?

These were questions we still asked, but it was getting slightly easier to just shrug and let it go as time went on.

After all, thanks to Crimson Chaos—whoever he was, whoever sent him, however the whole ordeal came to be—Brock and I found our way back to each other.

Sure, maybe we would have found our way without spirits, a pain-in-the-ass ghost, creepy dolls in the freezer, and possessed old televisions.

But our story included a happy ending for Presley and Ren—or at least something happy after such a terrible loss—and we also got to forever recall the way we fell in love restoring our home.

Our home.

When Crimson disappeared, Bernard wasn't sure what to do with the house. We'd never been completely sure of their business dealings, but Crimson had paid us and kept Bernard in some extra cash without actually purchasing the home until he deemed it finished and ready to buy.

Which meant, upon his disappearance, Bernard had plenty of cash, we'd been paid *nicely*, and the home was just sitting pretty waiting for a buyer.

After about five minutes of discussion, Brock and I offered to take the place off Bernard's hands, and he gladly made us a sweet deal.

Shelton Contracting easily transitioned to Shelton-Mills Contracting.

We increased our radius of customers and never once had to worry about not having satisfying, paid projects to work on.

Brock refused to hire someone to clean the basement, so I had nightmares for months after the terrors we found down there.

Okay, it was mostly just spiders, dead rodents, and snake skins. Also, did I mention the spiders?

The worst part was moving the freezer out—truly, it was like moving a damn mountain.

Oh, and the dolls.

Those damn dolls.

If I never see another ventriloquist dummy again it will be too soon.

An antique collector who specialized in oddities came to see the collection. In total, the dummies brought in about three thousand dollars. The collector also paid a pretty penny for many of the items in the senior Presley's clinic area.

That money had been socked away for a vacation.

I had every intention to talk Brock into making it a honeymoon vacation very soon.

The first Halloween we'd celebrated in our new home—which we'd continued renovating to *our* specifications once Crimson was no longer making demands—we'd had a few trick-or-treaters thanks to parents willing to drive their kids all the way out to our place.

Brock had gone all out with the decorations, really playing up the theme of the haunted old house, while also making it fairly kid-friendly and welcoming.

Halloween and beyond brought visitors to see what we'd done with the place and we always enjoyed the stories they'd tell—passed down through their families —about the home and its occupants.

We didn't hear from Presley throughout the year, but last Halloween, he and Ren showed up under their tree. We'd spent a very nice stretch of time visiting with them. Presley was ecstatic with the final restorations and the children who came to trick-or-treat and visit the now-welcoming home.

"You think they'll come? Maybe last year was just a fluke? Maybe they're too busy or too far away," Brock whispered as we made our way toward the tree.

"I think if they're able to be here, they will be." Wrapping my arms around Brock, my chin over his shoulder as my chest pressed to his back, I took his hand and reached our fingers out to trace first the P hearts Ren, then the P and C, and finally the C hearts B 4-ever.

Brock sighed and turned his head for a searing kiss. "You taste like chocolate," he murmured against my lips.

"You taste like heaven and promises," I quipped back.

"Ohhh, pulling out the sweet-talking big guns," he teased.

A chilly breeze ruffled the sparse, dry leaves and a shiver traveled through me.

We turned as one and there they were.

Ren and Presley, standing before us almost as if they were visiting townsfolk just come for coffee and a looksee at the incredible hardwood floor.

"Hi," Brock breathed out. "Can you stay a while?"

Presley and Ren exchanged a glance and smile before nodding.

The next hour was filled with sweet stories of then and now, laughter, and letting Presley see just how filled-with-love his home was now.

All too soon, the men began to fade and we followed them from the house into the misty, moonlit night.

"Will we see you again?" Brock asked, taking my hand and pulling it around his shoulders.

Presley cocked his head to the side. "Most likely." He glanced up at the house, *our home*, and smiled. "Thank you for completing what Ren and I started here. A true home should be filled with love. Of family, of friends, of happy times."

"Thank *you* for being the reason we found our way back to each other," I said, my voice gruff with emotion.

"Your souls would have eventually met again," Presley mused, flickering in and out of sight. "Souls which are meant to be together will always find a way."

With that, he took Ren's hand and they walked off

into the night, disappearing beyond the veil. "Be happy," a voice whispered on the wind.

We turned to walk into the house.

Into our future.

Our happiness.

Our forever.

Second chance souls for the win.

Thanks to love and the ghost who saved us.

www.ingramcontent.com/pod-product-compliance
Lightning Source LLC
Chambersburg PA
CBHW030129260626
47156CB00008B/2864